BIGHT OF BANGKOK
A Collection of Short Stories

Bight of Bangkok is a collection of stories dealing with the raw underside of contemporary Thailand. It does not pretend to be pretty-pretty. In a country going through profound socio-economic and even psychological changes, there are many things which shock outsiders, not least the enormous disparity of wealth between the capital and the countryside. Thais have learned with good grace to accept these differences.

Michael Smithies retired from the United Nations in 1992 after spending 30 years in South-East Asia. He first came to the region in 1960 as British Council Education Officer in Thailand, and from 1964–65 was in charge of the British Council office in Cambodia; he subsequently taught in universities in Thailand, Hong Kong, Indonesia, Papua New Guinea and Singapore. Among his many other publications are *The Siamese Embassy to the Sun King*, which deals with Kosa Pan and Louis XIV, *Old Bangkok*, *Yogyakarta: Cultural Heart of Indonesia*, *A Singapore Boyhood*, *A Busy Week: Tales from Today's Thailand* (with Heinemann Educational, Singapore) and he co-authored the first major guide to Thailand, *Discovering Thailand*.

WRITING IN ASIA SERIES

Modern Malaysian Chinese Stories translated by Ly Singko and Leon Comber
Maugham's Malaysian Stories edited by Anthony Burgess
Twenty-Two Malaysian Stories edited by Lloyd Fernando
Son of Singapore by Tan Kok Seng
Man of Malaysia by Tan Kok Seng
Eye on the World by Tan Kok Seng
Three Sisters of Sz by Tan Kok Seng
Singapore Short Stories edited by Robert Yeo
Little Ironies: Stories of Singapore by Catherine Lim
Love Notes by Catherine Khoo
Curfew and a Full Moon by Ediriwira Sarachchandra
Or Else, the Lightning God and Other Stories by Catherine Lim
Foam Upon the Stream — A Japanese Elegy by Ediriwira Sarachchandra
The Adventures of Holden Heng by Robert Yeo
Web of Tradition by Woo Keng Thye
The Shadow of a Shadow of a Dream — Love Stories of Singapore by Catherine Lim
Honour and Other Stories by Goh Sin Tub
The Ghost Lover of Emerald Hill and Other Stories by Goh Sin Tub
The Nan-mei-su Girls of Emerald Hill by Goh Sin Tub
Hearts & Crosses by Nalla Tan
Encounter and Other Stories by Woo Keng Thye
Ghosts of Singapore! by Goh Sin Tub
Reflections in the River by W W Williams
More Ghosts of Singapore! by Goh Sin Tub
Winds of Change by Woo Keng Thye
A Dying Breed by Wong Swee Hoon
Malayan Horror by Othman Wok
Daughters of an Ancient Race by Jack Reynolds
Love's Lonely Impulses by Catherine Lim
Deadline for Love and Other Stories by Catherine Lim
Tales of the Hungry Ghosts by Judith Anne Lucas and Marsha Goh
Tapestry: A Collection of Short Stories edited by Helen Lee
Goh's 12 Best Singapore Stories by Goh Sin Tub
Lovers & Strangers by Robert Raymer
Sunshine in the Rain by Toh Weng Choy
The Best of Catherine Lim by Catherine Lim

BIGHT OF BANGKOK

A Collection of Short Stories

Michael Smithies

HEINEMANN ASIA
SINGAPORE

Published by
**Heinemann Asia, a Division of
Reed International (Singapore) Pte Ltd
Consumer/Education Books**
37 Jalan Pemimpin, #07-04/05, Block B
Union Industrial Building, Singapore 2057

OXFORD   LONDON   EDINBURGH   MELBOURNE
SYDNEY   AUCKLAND   MADRID   ATHENS
IBADAN   NAIROBI   GABORONE   HARARE
KINGSTON   PORTSMOUTH (NH)

*All rights reserved. No part of this publication may be
reproduced, stored in a retrieval system, or transmitted
in any form or by any means, electronic, mechanical,
photocopying, recording or otherwise, without the prior
permission of Heinemann Asia.*

ISBN 9971-64-316-2

© Michael Smithies 1993
First published 1993

Cover design by Cubes & Lines Design Pte Ltd
Typeset by Linographic Services Pte Ltd
using 10/13 Garamond
Printed in Singapore by Chong Moh Offset Printing Pte Ltd

Contents

Acknowledgements	vi
Preface	vii
1. A Life Lost	1
2. Bedblocks	10
3. Dog	22
4. Medical First	31
5. A Brand New Motorcycle	46
6. Ear Off	55
7. The Colonel's Lady	63
8. The Consul's Daughter	70
9. Child Divine	78
10. Miss Plastic Rose	86
11. Shotgun Marriage	100
12. The Drink-Mixing School	110
13. Welcome Home	117

Acknowledgements

The author would like to thank the *Bangkok Post* for permission to reproduce the story *Dog* which was originally published on Sunday, 11 December 1988.

Thanks are also given for the inspiration provided by articles which appeared in this newspaper on 20 July 1985, 21 August 1985, 20 March 1986, 18 July 1986, 30 July 1986, 31 July 1986, 9 August 1986, 20 August 1986, 21 October 1986, 2 July 1987, 5 July 1987, 15 July 1987, 16 July 1987, 28 July 1987, 30 July 1987, 6 September 1989 and 9 January 1992.

Preface

The grain that irritated the oyster producing each story in the *Bight of Bangkok* was in every case (with one exception, but which was also based on truth) a newspaper story reported in the English language press in Thailand in the last few years. In one case, it has to be admitted that three different stories have been telescoped into one. But all are true.

The settings of this baker's dozen have been altered, the names changed, and little here resembles the original characters, which are essentially recreations, except by unintentional coincidence. Any resemblance to persons living or dead is therefore entirely fortuitous.

Enough has been said about Thailand's charm, friendliness and fascination. Here, something of the underbelly of the country is shown. In a land which is developing extremely rapidly, there inevitably arise social tensions, and traditional values are eroded or distorted. These stories, based on reported events, may not always show particularly desirable aspects of the human character, but they illustrate some of the problems and contradictions evident to the most casual observer of contemporary Thai society.

Like many countries which have sought or recently have

had modernisation thrust upon them, Thailand has yet to adjust completely to the modern world. The contrasts between the old and the new are never far beneath the surface of society, and sometimes are all too apparent. Many pillars of the establishment have yet to come to terms with a society which has profoundly changed in recent years. Thailand is no longer a land of happy peasants tilling their rice fields. Many work, if at all, and at best, in factories or building sites in or near the capital for long hours and low pay. A number seek work overseas in labour-short countries. Their land is often sold or barren or both, and drought constantly haunts the most populous and impoverished parts. The sex industry flourishes, to the embarrassment of at least some members of officialdom. The temple has ceased to be the pivot of a rapidly urbanising class, in the same way as in the west where the church has become just a setting for certain life-cycle events.

Thailand is the Land of Smiles, according to the tourist promotion; of pollution, according to some tourists. The land with the second highest incidence of homicide in the world, or so it was reported a few years back. A land with a high incidence of HIV infection. But at least, all this is honestly admitted and taken in one's stride. That fatalistic streak — of accepting things as they are and making the best job of them — accounts for both *mai penrai* (not to worry) and the search for *sanuk* (fun). For, if one just looked on the gloomy side, life would indeed be intolerable.

A Life Lost

Somkiat had come to Bangkok from the north-east looking for a job, like many others from that impoverished region. He was totally unexceptional but was ready to smile in spite of the hardships life offered him. He had what passed for education in one of the remoter villages of the province everyone still calls Korat but which the government insists is the grander-sounding *Nakorn Rajasima*, city of the royal boundary stone. In other words, he attended primary school and, as well as learning to read and write and add his numbers, he also studied things like the names of the parts of a classical dancer's costume and a few words of a language called English which the teacher was quite unable to understand, much less teach.

His family was large and desperately poor. They had no land of their own left; it had all been sold, below market value, to the Chinese middleman from whom they had borrowed over the years and who finally foreclosed, putting the land in the names of the middleman's children who had been born in Thailand. The village had no assets; there was electricity, but fewer than half the families could afford to have a meter installed. There was no water, except what was hauled up in the morning and late afternoon from a large rain-fed pond, and which fairly regularly dried up towards the end of each hot season. Somkiat was the fifth of seven children. His one aim in life was to go to the capital, like his elder brothers and sisters, and work. He would try to save and send money back to his parents, who stayed because they were too old to do anything else, and who eked out a living catching fish in the village pond and hiring themselves as day-labourers on the tapioca farms when occasion arose. His mother also spun silk sometimes, and sold, far too cheaply, her products to passing merchants. There was no road in and out of the village, only a dusty rutted track which was completely impassable at times in the rainy season.

He was fourteen when he left school, borrowed some money for the bus fare, and with a friend, Uthai, who was also looking for work, went down the dusty track to the nearest district centre. There they took a bus to the capital, entirely unprepared for the world of work.

The clogged roads, leading into the city filled with everything from luxury cars to push carts, were the first signs that life there was entirely different from home. They knew something about it, from having watched a neighbour's television on occasions. They thought it was impossible that there could be so many cars and buses anywhere in the world. As they approached the bus terminal, the traffic got worse, so did the air, the trees got thinner and the buildings taller. Somkiat began to feel afraid. "I have to make it here, I have to. There can be no going back," he said to himself.

They got off the bus and were accosted by touts lying in wait. "Want a job? I can get you a good one." "Need somewhere to stay? No problem, come along with me." Somkiat had a peasant's caution, though. "No thanks, I'm staying with my brother." Fortunately, he had written to Godet and had been told to wait by the fountain inside a nearby shopping centre at about 8 p.m. on the appointed day. His brother was well aware that Somkiat had no idea how to get around Bangkok, and had thoughtfully told him how to get there after leaving the bus station. "Turn right outside the station and walk until you come to a big crossroads, with a bridge carrying a lot of traffic. Carry straight on. The first big building on the left, past the bridge, is the shopping centre. Go inside the main entrance with the steps and look for the fountain. I'll be waiting for you at 8 p.m. on Thursday, the day you come," his brother had written. As a precaution, he also gave Somkiat directions of how to get to his home if they failed to meet. It sounded very complicated.

It was just as well he had his instructions. Somkiat was right meat for a shark. And he was so afraid of being late that he arrived, together with Uthai, long before time. He had not expected the bridge Godet mentioned to be a road bridge over a road; he thought it would be over a canal or something. He was amazed by the crowds inside the shopping centre. Thousands of people, more than he had ever seen in one place before, were milling around, most smartly dressed, some less well so, and some extraordinarily. He was envious of their having so much money to waste on clothes.

Godet was true to his word, and came just before eight to collect his brother. Uthai had nowhere to stay that night either, so Godet told him to come along too. Godet shared a flat in Huay Kwang with several others from the same village. In theory, the flat belonged to an uncle, who no longer lived there, but they paid the rent, the water and the electricity bills, ate frugally on noodles or sticky rice and cheap fish, *pla too*, from any one of the many stalls nearby, and saved as much as they could after sending home each month what they could spare. The flat had two rooms; that night Somkiat and Uthai shared the space with fifteen others.

On the way to Huay Kwang, Somkiat asked Godet what he should do to find a job.

"What do you want to do?" Godet asked.

"Anything," replied Somkiat, truthfully, adding, "anything that's legal, that is. Are there any jobs where you work?" Godet worked in a shoe factory, cutting uppers.

"No, not really, and they wouldn't take on a close relative. I think you should walk around and look at construction sites. There are plenty these days. You look strong enough. They'll probably take you on. But don't expect to get the minimum wage right away."

"How much is that?"

"Just over a hundred baht a day now. But most employers don't pay it; they make deductions for this and that, keeping some back as a guarantee, they say. As you have no experience, you'll be lucky to get ninety. Some new arrivals only get board and keep until they know the ropes."

A Life Lost

With their friends, and talking dialect, they discussed this topic into the night after taking a shower.

Early the next morning Somkiat was up and washed his and his brother's shirts. Together with Uthai, he went down the garbage-strewn staircase smelling of urine from the fourth floor of the block, had a bowl of noodles, and went off, taking a couple of buses as his brother had told him. Godet had advised Somkiat to go to the Sukhumwit area, as there was a lot of construction going on, and just ask at sites. They did this systematically, starting where they got off the bus at Soi 1, doing the odd lanes first.

Somkiat was quite astonished at what he saw at times. There was a whole quarter which seemed to be full of Arabs and their female Thai partners. There were westerners everywhere, some walking hand-in-hand with girls barely old enough to be their daughters. The hotels seemed huge, the traffic on the main street dreadful. At Soi 17, he was told to come back the next day, as there might be a possibility, but they were not sure yet. Soi 19 seemed promising, and Soi 23 better. Somkiat gave up by the time he reached Soi 31, too tired to carry on. He was not daunted, and did not expect to find anything on his first day. Uthai carried on, and his patience and perseverance were rewarded; he found something at a site, with very basic accommodation provided, when he got to Soi 35.

Somkiat returned to Sukhumwit early the next morning, and was taken on at the site of a block of flats in one of the lanes where he had been told to return the next day. He later found out this was a kind of endurance test;

they always did that. He was told he would get the minimum wage, less unspecified deductions for his protective clothing. This consisted of boots, gloves and a hard hat, all of which he had to leave at the site. His job was to do whatever he was told, mostly helping others on the site move equipment to where it was needed.

He liked work. He did not mind the hours, from seven in the morning to six in the evening. He did not mind the heat at midday or the rain when it came down in torrents towards the end of the day. He was soon promoted for his diligence, and put at the top of the giant sand and cement mixer. This took in graded sand and cement which were mixed, water added and churned until ready for pouring. The sand was piled high like a mountain nearby, with a division for each quality. A huge scoop gathered up the graded sand when required and put it in the cement mixer. Somkiat's job was to make sure the raw materials went straight into the mixer and did not spill over; he had to control the intake from a giant chute.

He saved hard, and was very proud when after two months, he was able to send five hundred baht home. He did this through someone who was going back to the village for a weekend, and sent a note to his mother:

Don't worry about me, Mum, I'm fine. I like my work. I stay at the flat with Godet. Uthai found work too and stays on site. I hope you are all well, especially Pa, Nit and Meo.

Nit and Meo were his two younger sisters, still remaining at home to complete their schooling.

A Life Lost

On a wet afternoon in the rainy season, some three months after he started work, Somkiat was shouting something to his workmates at the bottom of the filter, when he slipped. He cried out, but there was nothing to hold on to. He fell straight into the open filter and was instantly crushed. The foreman on the site rushed to stop the machine, but it was too late.

Godet took no notice when Somkiat did not come back that night, and thought he had stayed with new-found acquaintances nearby the site. When he did not return the second night, he was concerned, and still more so the third. Fortunately he knew where Somkiat was working, and went to the building site. He asked what had happened to Somkiat.

"Somkiat? We've got no bloke by that name here," he was told. "Oh, just a minute. Are you a friend of his?"

"No, I'm his brother. He hasn't been home for three nights and I am getting worried. He's rather young still."

"You'd better see the foreman," said the guard at the gate. He went off to get him, unwilling to break the news himself.

The foreman came over, looking serious. "Bad news, I'm afraid." He was not a person to beat about the bush, and told Godet exactly what had happened. "There was nothing we could do. It happened all too quickly. We didn't know whether he had any relatives in Bangkok. The body was sent to the Poh Tek Tung Association."

Godet was stunned and did not know what to say or do.

"We'll give you his wages of course. And pay the funeral expenses. In your village."

Godet saw the trick. "He died here, he should be cremated in a temple here."

The foreman was sorry the ploy had not worked. Bangkok cremations cost more than twice those in the villages. Godet too wanted to avoid expense.

"As you like," the foreman replied.

"What about compensation?" asked Godet. "My brother died working for you."

"I'll have to discuss that with the boss."

Godet showed his mettle. "Have you reported his death to the police and the Labour Department?"

"Of course."

"In that case we don't need to discuss with the boss the question of compensation. How much will he give?"

"He'll settle for five thousand."

"Five thousand? Is that all my brother's life is worth?"

"That's all you'll get from this boss. Your brother had not been working here very long. You could try taking it to the courts, but the lawyers will eat up everything you might get, you know that. So five thousand, agreed? And you must sign a paper saying you and your family will make no further claims on his behalf."

Godet had been brought up to believe that it was useless arguing with those in power and authority. He took the offered compensation, and not only signed the guarantee (in front of two witnesses), but also signed a paper absolving the firm from blame for the accident which was attributed to the worker's negligence.

He went to his factory very late, and explained what had happened. He asked for a couple of days' leave to go home to tell his parents, and then arrange for the cremation in Bangkok. He was a good worker and was given permission to go. He took the night bus, stowing the money carefully in different parts about his person, and tried to avoid any contact with other people: he did not want to risk having a drug put in a drink and all his money stolen. The old woman next to him on the seat snored all the way. Godet tried to stay awake, but caught himself dozing off a couple of times. He had never carried so much money in all his life before.

But when he got home, he found he could not tell his parents that Somkiat, their youngest son who had left home so recently, was dead. And for the first time he lied to them. "Somkiat asked me to bring you this money. He's got a job in a Middle Eastern country, and said you won't be hearing from him for some time. Use the money carefully, he said."

The old couple cried in gratitude.

Bedblocks

"So high bed!" exclaimed the hot and confused young Japanese tourist to his recently-met lady companion as they entered the stuffy and rather sordid room in a cheap lodging near the main railway station.

Fortunately the air-conditioner was already on, its throaty gurgling drowning out the traffic noises from the polluted street below. Nit, which she said was her name, went over to the window and pulled the tattered curtains. "Someone see no good," she replied, with a recently-acquired nasalised accent she thought sounded rather fetching. Putting both hands on her hips, a provocative gesture she had seen a movie actress make on television, she took a come-get-me stance.

"Like drink?" she asked. There was a half-consumed bottle of Mekong on a tray with a couple of used glasses beside it. Plastic bottles of drinking water were also lined up on the table against the wall.

Fumio knew all about those Thai drinks, or so he thought. They slipped a pill in them when you were not looking, you woke the next morning feeling terrible to find you had no wallet. Foreigners were even doing it in Tokyo now. No, he was going to be careful, in spite of his thirst.

Bedblocks

"No tank. Me no tirty."

Even Nit realised there was going to be a communication problem; she was not sure whether he understood her question properly. She decided he was probably not in need of a shower. He was unlikely to find the grimy shared bathrooom with the squat toilet at the back of the lodging house up to overseas standards. Better get on with the business without further ado.

Even so, she rinsed both glasses, poured a little Mekong and water into each, and gave one to him. Fumio was watching intently, she could see.

"No worry, good," she said reassuringly, sipping a little from his glass before handing it over to him. Fumio became more relaxed, less because of the alcohol than because he had clearly seen there was no funny business, and she had drunk some of his mixture too. He placed four purple-coloured notes as advance payment on the small table beside the water bottles resting against the wall.

"Come, sit," she added, patting the bed affectionately. It was very hard, like most mattresses in the tropics, designed to reduce sweat. A floral print sheet in some need of washing covered it almost to the floor; a couple of pillows, in a similar state, rested against the bedhead.

Fumio did as he was told. He was already beginning to regret this little adventure, but this was his first trip abroad, and all his friends at the office had told him he must try it once in Thailand — it was very nice, and so cheap too. He had only met Nit an hour or so before, in the neon glare of a fast-food eatery where he had decided

Bight of Bangkok

to take his lunch, not trusting all those messy-looking curries, no matter how appetising they smelt. He did not really know how to start. The Japanese method was more like brutal rape, but he knew enough about his host country to realise a samurai attack might be counter-productive.

Nit could sense a hesitation. "No ploblem, we OK here," she said in her sing-song voice. Three years before, when she first came to Bangkok, she would not have known what to do next. A simple girl from a northern village, she had moved to the capital to find a job. Her education was minimal, her talents few. She had drifted into prostitution because it gave the biggest returns in the shortest time. She regularly sent money home and her parents had few illusions about how it was made. They asked no questions and at least had clear consciences, unlike many others in the village, who openly sold their daughters into prostitution. The concrete and brick house they were building with her savings was not a home that oozed blood-money at every interstice.

Expertly, she placed her hand on Fumio's crotch. He was already aroused. "You number one!" she said, as she did to all her customers, and unzipped his flies.

Imagination can supply most of the details of the succeeding minutes. Clothes flew off, a condom packet was ripped open (Nit took no chances), pants and a bra fell to the floor. On the disordered bed, a heaving pair coupled with grunts and moans that may or may not have indicated pleasure.

This doubtful ecstasy, after a climax had been swiftly

Bedblocks

reached, was interrupted by a rapid knocking at the door.

"Who's that?" Nit asked in Thai. A reply came — unintelligible to Fumio. Nit's brow furrowed. "My father he come see me. He go wait downstair. Quick, quick, you go."

Throwing Fumio's shirt and underpants at him, she gathered up her own clothes and quickly put them on, ignoring the sweat on her body and the inconvenience of having to maintain appearances. Fumio, in a state of panic increased by his unfamiliarity of the scene and local customs (would her father hit him, or make him marry her?), dressed even more quickly, slipped on his shirt, seized his trousers which had fallen to the floor, and ran his hand through his short hair.

"Go, go out front door, quick!" she said. He tried to hold her hand but she released herself, her duty done. "Quick, go. I go down after."

Fumio ran down the stairs as fast as he could checking his flies and tucking in his shirt as he went. Sitting in the corridor was a burly man he had not seen when he came in; he was either the father in question, or the house owner. He did not care to enquire, but nodded as he passed the man, and went into the freedom of the clogged street.

At first walking quickly, avoiding the usual obstacles on the pavement of hawkers, beggars, children playing, small tables and stools of the noodle vendors, fried banana stands, and car mechanics at work, Fumio gradually reduced his pace. His mind went over the whole, as he admitted to himself, rather sordid scene. Still, he reckoned, he had at least got value for money; the interruption could have come sooner.

Money. The power of the word. He was about to enter cloud nine of a philosophical abstraction concerning the evils of a world devoted to the acquisition of material things, when he stopped short, and felt his hip pocket. His wallet, from which he had taken those four fresh purple notes, was not there. Gone with it were at least thirty of its kind, several hundred dollars, and some yen as well, not to mention his visiting cards. Fortunately, he had been prudent enough to leave his passport and traveller's cheques deposited with his hotel, and, believing in thrift, he owned no credit cards.

Could his wallet have fallen out accidentally, he asked himself. Hardly, though it was just possible he had not fastened the button in the haste of the initial moments. He went over the whole scene again. He could hardly go back if the girl's father was really there and there would be all sorts of language problems. What was he to do? He was tempted to put it down to an experience and forget the whole affair. But there was a streak of righteousness in him which would not allow him to take the easy way out. He decided to report the matter to the police. If his wallet had fallen out, it could be returned to him; otherwise, justice could be done. He stood to lose nothing, he reckoned, and might even gain.

He asked in his broken English for the nearest police station. No one understood him, and a crowd of spectators soon gathered around him, several trying to help. A passing policeman on a motorbike noticed the crowd. Fumio saw relief at hand. "We go police station," he said. The young man on the motorised beat knew that tourists now formed the rice and curry of the country, and saw no obstacles to the request.

At the station, an English-speaking officer was called out of an air-conditioned office to interpret and take care of the case. He was hardly bilingual, but did his best. As Fumio recounted his misadventure, the police officer became more interested. This was the second time this week a similar tale had been recounted to him by a flustered tourist; the last was a Korean, who had refused to return to the scene of the alleged crime and the matter had lapsed. A fellow-officer had mentioned to him that a Bangladeshi had also reported a similar case. There was a curious consistency in them all: in all three, the room described had a high bed.

Police Lieutenant Boonsong was not very concerned about the morality of the case; his job was to enforce the law and make sure tourists were not overtly fleeced in the process. Here was a person who had manifestly been robbed — and in Fumio's case, of a considerable amount of money. He asked Fumio why he carried so much with him.

"But in Japan, we do always. There is no ploblem."

"This no Japan," Boonsong replied, falling into the idiom. "You take much money, you lose much money. Why you no use plastic card?"

"Per-las-tik?" Fumio reintoned after him. He thought for a moment, pondering on first the meaning and then the implications of the proposal. "No, I may owe money."

Bight of Bangkok

"But your way you lose money," Boonsong pointed out, in a matter-of-fact way.

Fumio could think of no appropriate answer. Perhaps for the first time in his stay in Bangkok, which had already run to four days, he felt that the other side was right. They were politely suggesting that what was normal in one place should not be done in another.

Boonsong could be decisive when the need arose. Calling a sergeant, he said to Fumio, "We go back to place you left, OK?"

"OK," agreed a rather humbled Fumio.

Their Suzuki jeep roared up to the erstwhile trysting place, which looked rather deserted. There was no sign of life downstairs. Fumio, his embarrassment increasing every moment, led the officer and the sergeant to the floor and door of his downfall. The sergeant knocked. No reply. He knocked again. Silence. He turned the handle. To his surprise, (he was already getting ready to heave his weight against the door) it opened.

There was no one inside. The curtains were still drawn, but, doubtless from economy, the wheezy air-conditioner had been turned off. Boonsong glanced around the room, taking in the glasses on the table against the wall, the crumpled floral sheet, the grubby pillows, and the high bed. He just pointed his finger to the bed, and his sergeant, throwing back the overhanging and greying sheet to reveal the four legs raised on wooden blocks, dutifully went down on all fours to inspect underneath. He came out with a half-empty bottle of Mekong, a drinking glass, an almost full bottle of soda, a greasy pillow, and some vaguely erotic literature of the comic variety.

Boonsong turned to Fumio. "Man which drank in this glass, he have your wallet."

Fumio blushed at the realisation of the way he had been duped. Most likely someone was under the bed the whole time Nit and he were copulating on it. Nit must have pushed his trousers onto the floor. The person under the bed had pulled them into his observation post, taken the wallet, and pushed them back into the general disorder of the room. He marvelled at the ingenuity of the scam.

"Ah-so," he said, sucking in breath between his teeth. "Ah-so."

Pol. Lt. Boonsong, if he had been inclined, could have enjoyed this moment of truth. He did not. He was not interested in Fumio's discomfort. The larger view prevailed. This was already the third time such an incident was known to have happened in his district, and the scene must therefore have been enacted on many more occasions without having been reported.

"OK, we find girl!" he said, with emphasis.

Fumio imagined prowling through a series of insalubrious establishments in the company of Boonsong in search of his wallet. He could not face it.

"No, we ask downstair first," he replied.

Boonsong was willing to humour him. He was, after all, a tourist, a Japanese and consequently a rich one at that. He sniffed at least a cash reward, perhaps even the promotion he had been seeking for so long. He told the sergeant to make a few enquiries down below while he

Bight of Bangkok

looked around the room a little more.

Underneath the mattress was nothing, and nothing on any ledge. There was, though, a photograph of a young couple, clearly not brother and sister from the embrace in which they were clasped, poked inside a dirty pillow case. "I think this your girl," said Boonsong, showing the picture to the by now very sweaty Fumio.

"Yes, this he," he agreed, with even less attention to English grammar than usual.

"Boy here is, maybe, man under bed getting wallet," Boonsong continued.

The enormity of the relationship stunned Fumio. "You mean, boyfriend there while I . . . ;" he did not know anything but an extremely vulgar word in English, which he did not wish to show was part of his vocabulary.

". . . while you on top," Boonsong helpfully completed the unfinished phrase for him. "Yes, you think strange. Maybe. But people do many thing for money. Live in city no easy. Maybe they need money for something special."

"Like wedding?" asked Fumio.

Boonsong wondered if he was joking, but saw he was serious. A wry smile fleetingly passed over his face. "Not they. They no kind who get marry. Maybe sick mummy up-country, young brother he become monk short time. Big party cost too much."

It was Fumio's turn to suppress a grin at this. "So what we do now?"

"We see how sergeant is get on with enquiry," he said, a little pompously, with a phrase picked out of a book.

They went downstairs. There, the fat man and the

sergeant were in animated conversation. Protestations of innocence sizzled through the air. Seeing Boonsong and Fumio, they broke off, and the sergeant reported his findings to his superior. Boonsong relayed the information in condensed form.

"He say she come in with many people. Every day. We wait. Maybe they come back soon. They is three peoples; one girl, two man. I think wait. Birds can come back to cage."

Fumio and Boonsong concealed themselves in a room to one side of the corridor, clearly the quarters of the fat man, who rented the building. He, under instructions to say nothing, resumed his position outside, reading a paper by the entrance from the street. The sergeant went out to park the jeep in a less obvious position and then joined them.

Before long, Fatty came into the room downstairs and gave a report. Boonsong relaid the information. "Her friend just come back. I think she come soon too."

A few minutes more of suspense. Fatty returned. Boonsong translated. "She go upstair, with *farang*."

"What?" asked Fumio.

"With western man," he learnt. Instructions were given to the sergeant and to Fatty. Boonsong waited a few minutes, and smoked a cigarette to pass the time. Fumio declined the offer of one.

"We go to bed," the police lieutenant then said with renewed decision. In other circumstances, Fumio might have been alarmed at the implications. He was told, as they tiptoed upstairs, "You wait outside door. Come in when I say. But first you knock on door like you heard before. Like her daddy."

Fumio knocked as he was told, as well as he could remember. A stream of expletives in Thai answered his call. Boonsong whispered to him, "She say you come too soon!" The sergeant heaved open the door, Fumio had a glimpse of huge white hairy buttocks quivering in mid-air over a pale brown form. Pol. Lt. Boonsong and his aide went inside, and the door closed on an exchange that sounded far from polite.

The pitch subsided gradually and Fumio could sense that the owner of the white buttocks had changed disputational sides; from being opposed to the police entry he now appeared supportive. The sergeant came out and called Fumio in.

Boonsong did the introductions. "He have same ploblem as you nearly have, and come to us," he explained to the hairy *farang* who had retrieved his trousers for the presentation. Nit, slowly dressing, was quiet; she showed no emotion other than boredom. Her friend taken from underneath the bed looked sullenly at the floor. "Now we wait for their friend. Her daddy. Please sit down." Fumio thought Boonsong was behaving as though he were a host at a formal government reception, which in a way, perhaps, he was. The sergeant left the room.

Enjoined to silence, the remaining five waited a little longer. Then came more knocking at the door, just like that Fumio heard on his time round. This was followed by a short scuffle, and the sergeant showed in another young man, younger still than the one relieved of his post beneath the bed.

"Daddy of lady," Boonsong explained to Fumio and the *farang*. "Her brother really. Right, that is all." He ordered Nit and her partner to finish dressing. "We go police station."

Mr Smith, as the westerner called himself for the occasion, looked rather worried. "All you do is make statement. That enough," Boonsong reassured him. Smith looked at Fumio.

"I guess I have to thank you. You are braver than me. Come, let's go and get the whole thing wrapped up."

Boonsong handcuffed the two men to each other and propelled them from behind, helped by Smith and Fumio. The sergeant handcuffed Nit to himself, and went ahead to the Suzuki. The group made a strange procession across the crowded pavement. Passers-by stopped to stare.

What happened to the threesome, Fumio never found out. Boonsong managed to recover most of Fumio's money from them, which Fumio then shared with the police lieutenant, for without him Fumio would have been penniless. Smith also rewarded Boonsong and his sergeant. Both visitors went off briefly to celebrate together their release at a nearby bar.

But a few months later reports came in of similar happenings in the seaside resort of Pattaya....

Dog

He never had a name of his own. He was just "Dog" to everyone. A childless Chinese couple working for an international organization in Bangkok, and living in a modest flat in a small block, took him in as a puppy. Like all puppies, he was cute, he was cuddly, he urinated all over the place, and, when not crying for his mother or food, he would be busily chewing anything his sharp teeth could come into contact with. He had a particular preference for the footwear of the domestic working in the first floor flat; she had to leave her sandals outside the door, of course, so she spent much time after Dog's arrival looking for one which he was invariably chewing in a quiet corner.

Fa-mei, who had wanted Dog from the start, was bored in her flat on her own. They did without a servant, but housework alone was not very satisfying. She did not speak English very well, and had only a few words of Thai, enough to get by in the market. She knew her husband's position at home would not be improved if they had children; cadres stood a better chance of promotion these days if they were childless. She led a bleak, uneventful life, chatting to two other childless

Dog

Chinese couples lodged in the same block, but being rather careful nevertheless about what she said; one never knew who might report what. Dog, as she decided to call him, was to be the object of her affection and concern.

Her husband, Cui, was always busy. He had to work hard at the office, he said, and sometimes came home late. Speaking good English, as well as French, and having a much better grasp of Thai than she, he had far more fun. He also rather liked the possibility of leading the good life. He had many contacts with local Chinese businessmen, and knew all about the prices of cars, new and old. He was often invited to dinners with them, on which occasions Fa-mei found herself still more on her own. Cui realised his wife must be bored. Through his contacts, he bought her a video player and arranged for the regular delivery of Chinese soap operas to the flat; however, most of them were in Cantonese, which she, being from the north, could not understand. Furthermore she thought them a little decadent. Cui, on the rare occasions he was home at weekends, rather enjoyed them; he thought they showed a life-style which was enviable.

Dog loved being made a fuss of. Fa-mei and Cui forgave him for the puddles he created with such frequent irregularity, they let him nibble their bare feet, however much it hurt, and when he was big enough he was allowed onto the sofa — providing there was his own towel there, otherwise his fawn hair showed too much on the deep burgundy covers. But, brought up to be frugal for themselves, they did not overindulge him with food. They fed him scraps, useless white rice with the odd chicken bone or vegetable. These were nowhere near enough for him, especially when he was still growing.

But Dog had a natural instinct for survival. The first time his master and mistress went out and left him to his own devices, he was bored too. He chewed as much of the servant's sandals downstairs as he could. He tried to play with the aged watchman, who chased him away. The watchman did not like him, he knew that, because he once made a mess on the stairs, just after they had received one of their rare washes. So Dog went back upstairs and howled outside his front door. That soon brought out the couple who lived in the flat next door; the woman, a Thai, was rather frightened of dogs, but Dog was too small then to frighten anyone. Her husband, a westerner, seemed to have a knack of controlling Dog. These two fed him, of course, and their scraps were tasty; they gave him milk, liver, pork, chicken skin, cake, bread (even with butter on it, just for him). Dog soon got into the habit of sitting outside their flat whenever he could, and getting a real meal. He learnt to make only a small sound, so his feeders would not be angry, and food would come. He also learned not to feed as ravenously as the first time, for if he was still hungry, they would always give him more, and provide something to drink as well.

Those two went out little, except occasionally on weekends. Noi remained home all day, Jim went out to work, but was usually back early. They hardly ever went out at night. Cui and Fa-mei went out more and more, together now, and were often back very late. They paid

Dog

less attention to Dog, who was increasingly left to his own devices. He would play with the other dogs in the dead-end street during the day, and with the children and their minders, but at night he was always inside the building, waiting, or eating the food provided by Noi or Jim. He rewarded them with much affectionate display, mostly in the form of putting himself beneath their feet as they tried to walk down or up the stairs, and which, to his surprise, seemed to annoy them.

Dog became sensitive to language. Cui had decided right from the beginning, perhaps because it was rather un-Chinese to keep a dog at all, to speak to him in English; his real reason for doing this was to encourage Fa-mei to use English more, and in this her husband calculated correctly. She followed Cui's example, and her increased confidence led her to listen to radio programmes in the language and to use it when with her husband's non-Chinese friends. Of course, Cui and Fa-mei usually spoke Chinese to each other, but Dog was Fa-mei's most regular English listener. Noi and Jim used English together, and by extension with Dog too. So in his simplistic way, Dog began to divide the world into those who spoke in English and Chinese, and those who did not. The first group he regarded as his friends, because they gave him food and fussed over him. Those who used another language either ignored him or gave him kicks or slaps, like the watchman and the owner of the sandals below.

Though without a proper garden to rummage in and with only the street for a substitute, Dog lived in a relatively cosy if limited world. This was suddenly shattered after a few months. Cui received orders to return at once; no reason was given. He did not know if he was going to be promoted, as Fa-mei had hoped, or if his liking of the good life had not received the approval of his superiors. Fa-mei was glad to be going back home, but Cui had very mixed feelings. They were told on a Friday afternoon they were to catch the Monday afternoon plane. They spent the weekend packing their not very numerous possessions. Hand in hand, they took a walk down the street when all was done on the Sunday, Dog following, watering worthy vegetation on the way. Their cases left on Monday morning, and they soon after. Dog was left to fend for himself.

There were always Noi and Jim, thank goodness, and even the watchman now felt sorry for Dog and gave him left-overs. But the owner of the building, who had never been keen on the idea of having pets there, saw his opportunity of getting rid of Dog. He asked the husband of one of the remaining Chinese couples in his small block what he intended to do with the animal.

"I guess I'd better look for a family to take him," he said. He did, but with no success: too many people lived in flats now. So one day he bundled Dog into his car, covering him with an old cloth so he would not see where he was going, and off-loaded him at a nearby market, where he calculated Dog might have a reasonable chance of surviving. It was a novel solution; most people would have taken Dog to the nearest temple and hoped that Buddhist charity would prevail.

Dog tried to find his way back home, but failed. There

Dog

were too many busy streets to be negotiated. He returned to the market, for at least some food was available. But every time he heard a foreign tongue, he rushed after the speaker, thinking it might be Cui or Fa-mei, always to be disappointed.

He had a brush with death one day when running after a foreign speaker. Squatting forlorn outside a shop selling meat and vegetables, he detected English being spoken across the street. Without a thought of anything else, he dashed across. A passing car slammed on its brakes, just catching his front right paw. There was a terrible noise of another car, unable to brake in time, crashing into that which had stopped. No one heard Dog's howl in the uproar. He limped away as best as he could. The bone seemed broken, the paw hung limply. He was never to use it again.

Even so, he was not an ugly dog; a half-breed, not too big and with an intelligent face. The arthritic old mother of a building supplies shop-owner, who, being only able to walk a little with a stick, spent much time sitting on a stool on the pavement in the late afternoons watching the world go by, spotted Dog. He was limping, like her, and she took pity on him. He showed himself indifferent, until she spoke in Chinese to a grandson helping in the shop, when he pricked his ears up and at once became more affectionate. That decided the grandmother; here was a poor dog abandoned by some Chinese, and it was her duty to help. Dog was taken in.

Grandmother was nothing if not efficient. She made sure he had rabies shots, she gave money to a grandchild to buy a collar for him, and he became her companion, not only in street-watching in the late afternoons, but in moving around the shop and the living quarters behind. Dog settled down; life was more restricted — he got used to his lame paw but could not go far on three legs. But at least life was tolerable; food here was assured, and so was shelter.

Dog still watched though. About five one afternoon, he recognised someone; it was Jim, walking by with Noi, from his old home. They had fed him when he had been hungry. He hobbled up and sniffed Jim's trousers. Jim looked down in astonishment and did not recognise the animal. Noi did, though.

"Why, that's Dog who used to live next door to us!" she said.

Jim remembered. "Of course, it is. What are you doing here?" he asked Dog, patting him on the head, and then stroking him. "Whatever's happened to his leg?"

"Looks as though he's had an accident," Noi replied.

For Dog, it was just like old times. They both fussed over him, and then indicated they had to go. "No, you stay there, you mustn't come with us," he was told. He had always obeyed them, and stayed, however regretfully, seeing his link with his past disappearing.

They were in a hurry to go to the shops before they closed. Among their purchases were some cakes to give to Dog on the way back, with a whole egg in it in the belief it would make him strong. It was dark when they were near the spot where they had seen him, but there was no sign of Dog. They looked around. Grandmother

Dog

was still sitting on her stool in the twilight; they did not know that she had observed them before. "Are you looking for the dog?" she asked. "The fawn one?" They said they were. "I saw you just now. He's inside there."

Spread-eagled flat among the building supplies was Dog, asleep, having eaten, probably dreaming. The shop owner asked, "You knew him before, didn't you?" They woke Dog up, who wagged his tail in anticipation. Had his dream come true? Would he be taken home? His disappointment was real when he only received his pieces of egg-filled cake. They fussed again and left him with his new owners.

For some days, they discussed Dog. Jim wanted to bring him in, Noi was reluctant; she was afraid of the trouble dogs cause — the extra work, the washing and grooming of Dog that would be necessary. Finally she agreed, overcoming her fear of four-legged animals. They would take him on. They squared the watchman beforehand, saying that Dog was grown up now and would make no more messes; they were sure the landlord would say nothing, as he only worried about the rent.

They went back by car a week or so later. There was again no sign of Dog. Grandmother was not there either. The shop was only partly open and lanterns with blue characters were hung outside. The owner looked downcast. "You've come to see Dog?" he asked. "He's gone." They asked where. "He died. He was killed when crossing the road with my mother. A big Benz came very fast down the road and hit them both. She had her bad leg crushed and died in hospital." His face became ugly, contorted with rage. "Damned murderer! I'd like to kill him too. It's just as well he's in prison, or I'd get him."

Retreating as tactfully as they could, the couple went back to their parked vehicle. Jim noticed that Noi rubbed her moist eyes. Saying nothing, he just put his hand on Noi's, who held it firmly. They returned in silence.

Medical First

"The first successful penis transplant in medical history has been performed at Saphan Kwai Hospital" — astonished readers of Thai newspapers read one day. Articles appeared with almost complete details about the operation and the patient, who then fell out of the news. The real story behind the headlines was a tragicomedy.

The patient was an ordinary enough person. Boonmee was twenty-two years old and had joined the army to do his national service a year before. National service in Thailand is selective; not everyone has to do it, and the services decide how many people they want each year, rejecting those unfit or considered too small. Boonmee had not waited for selection; he volunteered to join the army. His parents were peasants from Chainat, with totally insufficient farming land to support all their children. Boonmee had dropped out of secondary school and had drifted into the capital and a succession of poorly paid jobs. As he saw it, being in the army would at least ensure he was fed and housed, and he would probably be taught something useful. He did not mind the rigours of military training and resolved to stay in for as long as he could.

Bight of Bangkok

Boonmee was not only very fit, he was also very good-looking. Back in his village, he had had plenty of successes with the girls, and in Bangkok he attracted a lot of attention. He had a series of affairs, more or less, just before he was called up, and before settling down with Pranee, who, for the sake of formality he called his wife. As with many couples, there was no registration, no wedding, not even a big meal in a restaurant; they cohabited in a rented room, and that was enough.

Pranee came from Samut Prakarn, now a suburb of the capital, where she worked shifts in a textile factory, earning much less than the legal minimum which itself was barely enough to survive on. Boonmee was certainly not her first boyfriend, but was the first one she had really cared for. She relished his dark good looks, his broad smile, his muscular frame. But she worried she might lose him too; she was well aware that female heads turned when Boonmee walked into a room, and she knew enough about his past to make her jealous. He was a *chao chu*, a ladies' man, and she had to be on her guard. She went to fortune-tellers and took the charms and potions the soothsayers gave her to make him stay faithful to her. She slipped some of their brews into his food when the occasion presented itself, hoping they would have an effect on Boonmee.

In spite of all her efforts, Pranee was not the only person who might pass for Boonmee's wife. Boonmee's idea of cohabitation was to stay with someone who gave him satisfaction, and he was a generous person with his personal favours. However, on weekends, he usually drifted back to Pranee. His frequent absences infuriated Pranee, who had not the same open-heartedness. They started to have rows, which became more bitter as they became more frequent. Boonmee soon forgot them; Pranee did not.

Once Boonmee joined the army, he had to stay in barracks during the week, and could only return to their rented room on weekends. He was not even very punctilious about that. He rather enjoyed his regained personal freedom; he took to spending Friday evenings with the boys, his mates, and not returning to Pranee until late Saturday morning, or even later, if a pretty face showed interest in him. During the week there was the usual barrack-room horseplay, which Boonmee, an easy-going sort, joined in. Some of it involved displays of physical strength and abilities. Boonmee's anatomical make-up was the envy of all, and he became rather proud of it, something he had not thought about before. He qualified for the nickname *Yai* (Big), given by his mates.

His army duties, his evenings with his mates or with newly-acquired girlfriends did nothing to improve his relations with Pranee. He took to returning on weekends even later, and once he skipped entirely when a fair face retained his attention for the whole weekend. The following week, when he had a pang of remorse and went back fairly early, Pranee miscalculated, and rewarded him with a blazing scene, which ended with her saying,

"You just chase after other women and leave me by myself to pay the rent, keep things clean, and wait for you to return."

Bight of Bangkok

"Well, if you don't like it, you know what to do," Boonmee replied.

At which Pranee broke down in tears. What could she do with this impossible philanderer, whom she loved, but at the same time realised she had begun to hate?

The following Friday evening was also the end of the month. Over a few bottles of beer in a nearby restaurant, Deng, one of his mates, started urging Boonmee to apply his charms to a pretty waitress.

"Look at her, she's not bad, you know. Nice figure, well-developed breasts. Something to hold on to."

The waitress, no novice to the attentions of soldiers from the nearby barracks, winked, but then pretended not to notice them. She was rather taken by Boonmee, though. Deng went up to her and whispered something in her ear. Whatever it was, it caused her to blush, and her interest in Boonmee to be renewed.

Deng returned looking pleased with himself. "She finishes work at 11.30 and is free this evening. Her name's Eek."

Names, names, what do they matter, thought Boonmee. He had enough beer in his stomach not to worry about anything in particular, and enough money in his pocket to pay for a cheap hotel for the night. What was more, he had Monday off, having done some extra guard duties during the week. Deng and his friends sat it out to keep him company; they left just before 11.30, and Eek soon appeared. Being nothing if not discreet, Deng and the others withdrew to the barracks.

Discretion also requires that little is said about the rest of the evening, except to say that both Boonmee and Eek

Medical First

enjoyed it considerably. But Boonmee was not in a position then to realise the disastrous consequences of his little adventure.

Boonmee and Eek were about to part the next morning after eating their raw eggs in condensed milk, washed down with Chinese tea at a roadside stall, when Eek asked what her stud was doing that day.

"I'm going home to Samut Prakarn. I guess I have to see my wife," he told her. Eek was not the jealous type, but was looking forward to the chances of a repeat performance.

"I'm free until this evening," she said. "Why don't we spend the day together?"

"Where?" Boonmee asked, not wishing to pay out more to so-called cricket hotels than necessary.

Eek knew it was impossible to take Boonmee back to the room which she shared with three other girls, but she had her connections.

"I've a friend who'll let me use her place during the day while she's out at work. It's quite near."

Boonmee was nothing if not compliant. "OK, let's go there then."

"What'll your wife say?"

"I'll tell her I had to do some extra guard duty."

They went off to Eek's friend's place, stocking up, after getting off the bus, on food from street stalls — fried chicken, mangoes with sticky rice and coconut cream (it was the hot season, with fruit as the only compensation for the soaring temperatures). Eek's friend lived in a squalid one-room flat on the top floor of a concrete block standing in a sea of garbage, used plastic bags and stagnant water, like all the other blocks in the same part of Huay Kwang. Eek obtained the key from some neighbours, who knew her and knew she had the occupant's permission to use the place from time to time. Boonmee and Eek were soon installed and enjoying themselves.

The real world intruded later. Eek had to go to work at five, and Boonmee had to return. He could not decide whether to go to the barracks or to Pranee. He had a crumpled shirt and he was tired from his exertions. He finally made up his mind to spend the night in the barracks, ignore the taunts of his envious colleagues, have a good sleep, put on a clean shirt, and go off to Samut Prakarn the next morning.

Pranee was waiting for him when he arrived before noon on the Sunday. He was still a bit weary, and she was exhausted from a week's slavery in the factory, as well as anxious about his absence the day before.

"What happened?" she asked.

"I had to stay on for extra guard duties. But I've got tomorrow off instead."

"Pity I'm at work then," Pranee answered.

They dispensed with formalities of greeting. There was nothing unusual in that. But Pranee's sixth sense told her that Boonmee had been out on the tiles. It was unlikely that traces of the cheap scented soap provided by the hotel or used at the Huay Kwang flat lingered, but Pranee saw the lines under Boonmee's eyes, noticed his glazed look, his apparent lethargy. Something had happened, she knew. She said nothing but watched.

Medical First

A noodle seller came by, ringing on the side of his dish. She went outside and bought their lunch. Boonmee took off his shirt and trousers, put on a *paakaomaa*, and went out for a shower. They ate silently on the straw mat on the floor in front of the television. Food over, Pranee curled up against her man, whose vigour had returned, and it was not long before they were locked in their wonted connubial postures.

It was when they were resting after their exertions that she saw the great love bite at the base of his neck which confirmed all her suspicions.

"He did not get that from one of his mates in the barracks, I'm sure," she said to herself. "Who was the filthy whore?"

Pranee had been waiting the whole week for a reunion with her hulk of manhood, whom no one was going to take from her. She was furious, furious with the unknown woman, furious with herself for depending on him, furious with him for his continued infidelity, and furious with him for lying to her. She sat down at their only table, her head propped in her hands, staring into space beyond the television set. Slowly a plan formed in her mind. She would do what many Thai women have done in such circumstances — she would stop the trouble at its source.

Pranee prepared the evening meal while Boonmee slept. He woke about five, feeling much better, and rose to take a shower outside, pecking at her as he passed. She suppressed a frisson of distate but he did not notice.

They ate their meal in silence — conversational silence that is — they usually did, while the television blared a thousand advertisements at them showing homes they could never afford, cars they could never buy, airlines they would never take. But the soft drink and shampoo advertisements, though set in luxurious surroundings, they could begin to relate to.

As Pranee cleared away the meal and prepared for the night, she asked, "Had a hard week?"

"Oh yes, tough."

"Go anywhere special?"

"I went out on Friday with my mates."

"Anything else?"

"No, nothing. Why?"

"I just wondered, that's all."

Boonmee flicked through all the four stations they could receive on their set, and found nothing but ads. He yawned, stretched, went out to brush his teeth, and lay down waiting for Pranee to join him on their mat which served as a bed.

She also went out, washed, and busied herself with some minor domestic matters while he dozed off. Then she joined him. Habit being strong, they were soon again consummating their marriage. Boonmee's animal strength was unabated, but Pranee played hard to get, inspiring him the more. Both exhausted by all this activity coming at the end of a week's work, fell into a deep sleep.

Pranee rose as dawn was breaking, Boonmee still sleeping soundly. She packed a small bag of clothes for herself, opened the door in readiness, went to where the kitchen things were kept, took out a carving knife, and returned. Removing Boonmee's loincloth, and holding up

Medical First

his inert penis, she took a decisive swipe and cut it off, throwing it out the open window.

Boonmee screamed for all he was worth, in severe pain, blood flowing everywhere. Neighbours soon came in through the door which Pranee had left open on her hurried departure and were astonished at the sight they saw. A quick-witted man among them guessed what had happened, and dashed off in search of a *samlaw* to take him to a hospital. The men tried to comfort Boonmee and to staunch the flow with ice cubes produced by a neighbour. The women murmured among themselves, "He got what was coming to him."

The *samlaw* raced to the city centre and towards the large hospital at a major crossroads in the middle. It was just past eight in the morning by the time they got there. The resident surgical team was debating whether to agree to a request from a homosexual who wanted a sex change operation, when Boonmee's case was reported to them. The chief surgeon called for order.

"Gentlemen, we have a unique opportunity. One patient wishes to have his penis removed, another has had his removed against his will. We are given the chance to reconcile the two. It will not be easy, and two delicate operations will have to be performed almost simultaneously. Are we agreed to try?"

There were general murmurs of agreement; there was little to lose. "What about tissue compatibility?" asked one of the team.

"I've thought of that; we can only hope."

"The same for blood grouping?" asked another.

Bight of Bangkok

"Fortunately most people around here have the same group; I repeat, we can only hope."

Boonmee, who had been given sedatives, was immediately prepared for his second operation that morning, and they told the waiting transvestite, to her obvious joy, that her unwanted appendage would be removed forthwith, and that she should be prepared to stay in hospital at least a couple of weeks. But for practical reasons the operation had to be performed at once. She was delighted to consent.

The team of doctors worked hard and long. The chief surgeon's hopes were justified; the blood grouping was compatible and so was the tissue. For seven hours, they struggled with knives, forceps, clips, sutures, and peered through microscopes at bloody ligaments. Anaesthetists checked their machines and nurses brought sterile instruments as required, carried out blood transfusions and cleared up the mess. At last it was all over, the patients were wheeled out towards the wards, and the chief surgeon took off his gauze mask.

"Well, gentlemen, it was hard but interesting work, I think. Microsurgery joining blood vessels is never easy. While we have probably assured the urine ducts in both donor and recipient, I am less sure about the sperm ducts in the recipient. Still more uncertain is the erectile quality of the recipient. Again, we can only hope." He was an eternal optimist.

Boonmee spent more than a month in the hospital, and of course got to know Ping, the donor who had offered him some hope, quite well. The hospital authorities

Medical First

were a little doubtful of the propriety of allowing the two to meet at first, and indeed were undecided whether to put Ping in the women's or the men's ward, but finally decided Ping would be classified as what he was when he went in, and no harm could come of their meeting. Boonmee was undeniably grateful, and tried hard to understand why Ping should not want his birthright.

"I've always hated myself for being what I am, or rather what I was," Ping told him. "I only ever thought of myself as a woman, I loved clothes and dressing up. And I love men, real men like you."

"I'm not sure I am a real man any more," was Boonmee's reply, "but if I am, it will be thanks to you."

They took to going around the hospital grounds together when they were able to move independently. Boonmee healed much more slowly, and still needed to be in a wheelchair most of the time. They compared notes on their progress, and discussed their after-hospital-plans.

"I'm going to give a big party for all my friends. You'll come, won't you?" Ping asked.

"Of course, if you think it would be all right," Boonmee replied. "But I don't know what to do yet. I'll stay in the army of course, until my time is up."

"What about your wife?" asked Ping.

"If I ever see her again, I'll kill her."

"That will put you in jail, not in hospital," was Ping's pragmatic reply.

"True, but I can't forget what she did to me."

"But things may be all right now," Ping said.

"Maybe. But what happens if it does not work as it should?"

Bight of Bangkok

"The doctor told you that there are now special devices developed in America during the Vietnam War for wounded veterans who had trouble like that. It'll be all right, don't worry. Find a new wife instead."

"A woman might laugh if she saw the mess down there."

"Then don't let her see it. Switch off the light. Say you're shy. Use your imagination."

"I don't seem to have as much as you. Will you get married after your party?"

"I hope so," was Ping's reply. "It's what I've always wanted, a man of my own. I'll have to get a new job; I can't carry on working at a transvestite bar any more. I'll try to be a secretary. I can type."

Boonmee followed his own train of thought. "I guess that's what my wife, my ex-wife that is, wanted too. A man of her own."

When things seemed to be working safely for both of them, the hospital gave a press conference. "Our success will be reported to medical bodies worldwide as part of an information exchange," the hospital director announced. The chief surgeon described the operation in technicalities. "The organ was removed from the homosexual as part of a routine sex-change operation, and implanted two centimetres into the recipient's pubic area," he said proudly, rather like a father. "The penis is in good condition and has grown new tissue. Later, part of the skin from the scrotum will be grafted onto the organ."

Those plans never came off. Boonmee returned to the barracks when he was well enough, but his fame had preceded him. Everyone wanted to see what a good job the hospital had done.

"Looks a bit of a mess to me," one said.

"Hey, Gay Dick, can you get it up?" asked one of the more vulgar.

"Is it going to stay like that?" asked a third, simply curious.

Yai, whose nickname was now less appropriate, chose to answer only the last question. "No, they're planning to do some more skin grafting."

"Wish you luck," replied his sympathetic mate.

"Did anyone find the original?" asked yet another onlooker.

Boonmee sighed at the recollection. "No. Our neighbour keeps ducks . . . ." He did not have to continue; events of this kind had ceased to make news in Thailand.

The army authorities were sympathetic. Boonmee was put on very light duties and was offered an honourable discharge if he wished to take it. He deferred a decision, not knowing what to do.

As the weeks went by, it became increasingly clear to Boonmee he could not continue his former life. His vigour was gone and his character had changed, becoming rather introverted. Ping kept in touch and felt sorry for him. Boonmee took her out to the cinema one evening; over snacks beforehand, Ping asked, "How are things down there?"

"Not so bad, but not the same. I have little interest in things now."

"Have you tried?"

Bight of Bangkok

"Not really. I'm afraid now. And I can't stay on where I am."

Ping could understand why. "How about going to the place where I used to work? They might have a job for you. I've been back once. All the 'boys' were delighted to see me, and many were very jealous."

Boonmee felt they could afford to be, especially as Ping, as a real woman, was very striking. "All right. When?"

"Now. We can go to the movie another time."

So they went instead to the Patpong area. Ping was given a tumultuous welcome. She introduced Boonmee to the patroness, who was at once struck by Boonmee's looks, and felt very sorry for him. She knew all the details, of course, from Ping. Boonmee was offered a job as a doorman and bouncer, and if he wanted to take on customers as well, that was his affair. "But they don't usually come here for your type," she warned him.

It would be tempting to be untruthful here, to say that Ping and Boonmee got married and lived happily ever after, or to report that Boonmee moved from outside to inside the bar and assumed a transvestite role within. Neither happened. Nor did Pranee ever reappear. Ping certainly remained a good friend to Boonmee, and eventually married a respectable banker. Boonmee remained on the outside of the door of the bar. But from being an easy-going extrovert, his operations seemed to make him passive, and he had far more successful encounters with would-be clients than the mama-san had bargained for. She turned a blind eye, for he was good at his job and good for business.

No, he was not taken off to Germany by a pot-bellied

farang. He occasionally got as far as Pattaya, and once even to Phuket, in company. He is still around at his job, though with the years his looks are not all they were. You can see him most nights at his station. His expected role in the annals of medical history was unfortunately not realised. There were, as they say, unforeseen complications.

A Brand New Motorcycle

Suwit was a fairly ordinary person living in the province of Prae. He owned rather less than 20 *rai* of land, not quite enough to make much profit from, with rice alone, but he was not entirely devoid of business acumen. He chatted with people, found out what was selling well and what was not. He planted small sweet corn at the right time, and made a good profit, before everyone else in his village caught on to the idea. He attended village meetings and heard all about planting secondary crops and trees along the paddyfield edges. Most simply nodded, went away and did nothing. But Suwit did as he was advised, put beans in after the rice had been harvested, lined his fields with coconuts, peanuts, *lantau* trees, limes, and did quite well in secondary lines. In many ways he was a model farmer.

His wife, Somsong, was an indulgent person; she let Suwit have his head, and carefully salted away the money that came in from selling off their cartloads of rice and all the extra crops that Suwit took a fancy to planting. She nagged at him to buy more land, so that they could increase their capital as it were (she did not use the term, of course). But her husband would shrug his shoulders;

A Brand New Motorcycle

he was keen to make money, but not if it involved great effort on his part. Extra land would undoubtedly require that. He got out of the difficulty by claiming there was none for sale in the village; it was not true, and his wife knew it, but said nothing to upset him.

Somsong and Suwit had three children who had survived the rigours of village life, all grown up now (several had died along the way). Their eldest, a son, on whom Somsong pinned all her hopes, had at first helped in the fields. He had spent a whole *pansaa* or lenten period as a monk in the temple, and his mother was radiant at the thought of a better afterlife because of the merit obtained from this devotion. But Prasong had his mind set on other sights: the village seemed too small, and after a time he managed to get his parents' agreement for him to go to Bangkok and to try his luck there. He had seen in a daily which specialised in advertisements in the "Jobs Offered" column, a bar called Saturn which sought at least 40 young men, who had to be 170 cm tall, between 18 and 25 years old, well-built, sporty and good-looking, which offered a monthly salary of Bt. 8,000 to Bt. 10,000 a month. This was almost as much as his father earned in a year from all his work in the fields, and he was considered well-off because of his successes in sidelines.

So Prasong went off to try his luck in the city. He must have done well; at first he sent money home fairly regularly, but gradually it tapered off, as did his visits for the new year, Songkran and other festivals; they saw less of him, and heard less.

Bight of Bangkok

That left the two girls, Kamonporn and Nowalak, at home. They were not particularly pretty by northern standards, but they were not hideously ugly either. They had, like their brother, gone through primary school and learned remarkably little. No one could accuse them of being intelligent. They would, in the course of time, find husbands and produce lots of children, mostly unwanted. Their father thought little of them; he took an almost Chinese attitude, that girls were there simply to be married off, and could not be considered an asset.

Chatting to friends in the district town one day, though, he realised he was wrong.

"Do you remember old Deng, from Baan Nok Keo?" asked one of his drinking partners. "You know, Deng with the squint?"

"Oh yes, of course," replied Suwit. "What happened to him?"

"He's become ever so rich. Bought some more land, got a motorbike, and they say is even thinking of buying a pick-up."

Such wonders of the modern world were in the realm of television ads, but not in real life as far as Suwit was concerned. "How did he manage that?"

"Well," and here his interlocutor looked around the coffee shop to make sure only their small group was listening, "they say he sold his daughter to Mother Prissana."

"Prissana? You mean the owner of the whorehouse by the river?"

"Her."

"And how old was his daughter?"

A Brand New Motorcycle

"Not too young. About sixteen maybe. But very pretty. And . . .", with another glance around the shop, "she was a virgin."

One of their small group, with perhaps rather more Mekong in him than was desirable, bawled out, "Not many of those left around here." The others looked at him in distaste. He quietened.

The little party came to a natural end shortly afterwards, as the bottle of Mekong was empty and no one had any money, or sufficient credit, to buy another.

Suwit went home on his bike along the dark, rutted laterite surface, occasionally nearly falling off as he sank into sand or came upon some fallen branches. He was not befuddled though. He was thinking hard. Why should he not have a motorbike too? Why should only some qualify for such a prestigious possession?

He got home without difficulty — the route was familiar enough, since he covered it at least twice a week — and, after a quick shower, crawled beneath the blanket beside Somsong. She woke briefly when he appeared, and was prepared to drop off again, but Suwit started a low conversation, telling her what he had heard.

"Why are you telling me this?" she asked. "What do you have in mind?" She knew perfectly well, but wanted him to come out clean.

He did not do so directly. "We are not like the head teacher and the village headman; they can afford motorbikes with their government salaries. But we, we who work hard and are considered successful, have little to show for it. We ought to have a motorbike too."

Bight of Bangkok

Somsong was a practical woman. They might have a new house as well, in time, with cement walls and a corrugated iron roof, perhaps even tiles. "You must have their agreement though," was all she said, and turned her back to snore loudly in resumed slumber.

Suwit worked at fulfilling the condition. He explained to Kamonporn and Nowalak that the family was poor, and now they were grown up (they were respectively 17 and 16), it was time they thought of contributing to the cash income of the family, and so on and so forth. He implied there were easy ways of making money, but one needed support.

The girls might be stupid but they could see what he was getting at. They discussed the matter between themselves.

"Why not, if it keeps him quiet? We could try it for a year, but after that our earnings are ours." The formula seemed fair.

So one day, cutting in on his usual blethering, Kamonporn, as the elder, said, "All right, dad, we know what you want. We'll do it for a year to repay our debt to you and mum as our parents. But after that, we choose what to do, and where we go." Suwit praised providence and the gods for giving him such practical offspring.

He cycled off to see Prissana and a deal was fixed. The two girls would spend a year at her command, and in return he would get a brand new 125 cc motorbike.

Soon after, Suwit was to be seen everywhere in the district town, in all the nearby villages, on his new red bike. He rode around for the sheer pleasure of it. Somsong

A Brand New Motorcycle

was pleased on his account, especially when she learned that Prissana had decided to send the two girls off to Bangkok; at least people might not make comments with them away from the district.

But after a few months, the villagers noticed that Suwit was rather bad-tempered, and his red motorbike was not to be seen. Suwit gave out the machine was no good and had gone in for extensive repairs.

But discreet enquiries then revealed he had gone to the police and filed a complaint against Prissana, accusing her of luring his daughters into prostitution. The police, who largely turned a blind eye to her activities, especially as she was said to provide them with free services from time to time, could not ignore a formal complaint, and were duty-bound to make enquiries.

When Smarn, the most senior local officer, called on Mother Prissana the morning after the complaint had been lodged, and with whom his relations had always been cordial, indeed close, he found a fury in front of him.

"That little runt! He dares accuse me of making prostitutes of his rotten daughters! Some say we are the oldest profession; we are also an honourable one! If we make a deal, we stick by it...." She went on to give graphic details of what she meant by a deal and how it would be adhered to. "Your little shit of Suwit made a deal with me, and the deal fell through. Not of my doing."

Smarn asked her to be more precise.

"We agreed his daughters — ugly little biddies they are really — would work for me for a year. In return, I would buy him a new motorbike. The model, the colour, the cc were all agreed between us. Fine. He brings along those bitches, Kamonporn and Nowalak, of their own free will mind you, and I hand over the bike. I didn't pay cash, of course. Where would I find it?"

The police officer assumed the question to be rhetorical. Everyone in the district knew Prissana was rolling in money. But she was a businesswoman first and foremost.

"I bought the motorbike with a downpayment, and was to pay back in twelve instalments, covering the twelve months those girls of his were to work for me."

"But he accuses you of making prostitutes of his daughters," said officer Smarn.

"He made them himself. I tell you, they came of their own agreement. No funny business. But he asked, for the sake of his reputation," she snarled at the word, and repeated it, for emphasis, "his reputation if you please, that they be moved out to Bangkok."

"Well?"

"Not well. I sent them to a brothel I know, a good place, very well run; the owner is an old friend. Good clientele, though rather busy. Very fancy in some ways, you know, see-through glass panel, numbers on all the girls." Smarn did indeed know, but let her continue.

"Those two found the work too hard or something, I'm not sure what. They weren't chained to the bed or anything. No kinky stuff either; just good straightforward sex, though perhaps some of the customers might be a bit demanding; we get them like that here too sometimes. Well, they found the going too tough, used to easy country ways, and came running back home."

A Brand New Motorcycle

"Back home? To Baan Nok Keo?" Smarn asked.

"Yes, I bet your pretty Suwit didn't tell you that, did he? They went back home, and told some cock-and-bull story about having been forced to go to Bangkok. I didn't force them. They asked to go themselves. I told them, OK, go if you want, but you still belong to me for a year. They agreed, fine. And then they run away. After five months."

"So what did you do?"

"Naturally I stopped payments on the motorbike. The motorbike shop called the vehicle in. And Suwit went back to his old bike."

Smarn thought a while, insofar as he was capable of thought. He knew Mother Prissana well enough to know she was probably telling the truth. He decided to mete out justice even-handedly.

"Mother Prissana, this is difficult. I must be seen to be fair. I'll have to book you both for procuring."

A look of astonishment crossed Prissana's pallid face.

"But don't worry," Smarn added quickly. "We'll get the lawyers to fix things up. We can fix bail at . . . shall we say . . . Bt.100,000?"

Prissana's eyes opened wide. "And where do you think I can get that from?" she asked.

"Come off it, Pri. The bank manager told me only the other day you had plenty more just sitting in your savings account." There were no secrets in the provinces, and precious few professional ethics either.

The whorehouse owner said nothing, thus indicating assent. That at least would fix Suwit, she reckoned.

Bight of Bangkok

The formalities were soon over, the money deposited. But Prissana could hardly believe her eyes the next day when she saw Suwit walking around town. She rushed to the police station.

"Can't you keep a deal either?" she snarled at poor Smarn. "I've just seen Suwit. In the street."

"I'm sorry. But his wife, Somsong, came in with the money. All in ten and twenty baht notes. It took ages to count. She agrees to get Suwit to drop the case if you agree to let him pay the remaining instalments . . . ."

Prissana cursed the cow under her breath. No point in wasting money with lawyers. The couple obviously had more than she had reckoned. She calculated quickly the losses (seven months' unpaid services) against the gains (no further payments, no trouble with lawyers or the police).

"Agreed. But this deal we stick to, eh?"

Smarn replied unctiously, "I'm sure I can persuade them to do that. So, complaint withdrawn."

And Kamonporn and Nowalak? They found life so boring back in the village that after only a week or so, they went back to the bright lights of the capital, from where they, like their elder brother, started sending money home.

Suwit not only got his red motorbike back, but Somsong called in a builder to start on the new house.

Ear Off

Prapart Chitrapoon thought he heard a strange noise. He opened his eyes. It was still dark. Next to him his sloppy wife of many years was sleeping soundly, snoring slightly. He listened carefully. In the distance there was the low muted roar combined with the occasional cock crowing. Bangkok was already beginning to wake up, the traffic was starting to circulate before becoming hopelessly jammed. He guessed it was about five in the morning.

There it was again. This time he was sure he was not dreaming. It sounded like someone moving around downstairs. He listened intently. His heart beat faster and seemed to make far more noise than it should. Yes, there was definitely someone there. Only one? He was not sure. Maybe not.

He wondered what to do. His mind raced. The telephone was downstairs in the living room, and in any case had been out of order for weeks, so was doubly useless. He could shout, and maybe the intruder, one or many, would run away. But what if no one heard? The only other person living in the house was Wanee, a distant relative of his wife, Jae. Wanee did the cleaning and cooking for a pittance, but was older than they, and rather deaf as well. The neighbours would not hear. Those in the two nearest houses on either side ran their air-conditioners all night, and the other houses were too far away.

There was more than one for sure. He could hear them slowly climbing up the stairs. He prayed that Jae had remembered to lock the bedroom door. He decided to wake her. He put one hand over her mouth and pinched her ample backside. She opened her eyes in astonishment. "There are robbers in the house," he whispered in her ear. "They're coming up the stairs. What shall we do?" Jae did not know whether to scream for help or faint, but instantly decided neither would be very useful. She quietly got off the bed and propped a chair under the door handle. Prapart retied his Chinese silk trousers round his waist and put his ear to the door.

He pointed to Jae, indicating she should line up against the wall near the door, and remain silent. He did likewise on the other side. Then there was a terrible scream. For a moment, Prapart was totally confused. He only understood when he heard Wanee's voice. "What do you think you are doing here?" she shouted at the intruders. She was already up and about to start work as usual; she certainly would not have heard the burglars.

"We've come for an early morning stroll," replied a rough male voice, speaking the language of the slums, "and we don't intend to add you to our haul, so shut up, you silly cow, or we'll shut you up good and proper." Wanee's reply was another scream, which was cut short in full flight.

Ear Off

"I told you we'd do it for you," the same voice continued. There were sounds of struggle. "For the last time," the voice continued, "are you going to be still or do I cosh yer one?" Prapart listened to the silence. "That's better. Now tell us where the money is."

A further silence ensued. Jae, on the other side of the door, showed signs of agitation. Wanee might indeed be a silly cow, in the accurate if inelegant words of the robber, but even so she was Jae's second cousin, and, though she treated her like dirt most of the time, she still had a sense of moral responsibility.

Prapart felt the time had come to act. Jae's chair would never keep the robbers from breaking down the door. Prapart, a comfortable civil servant who had never done much in his life, neither in work nor play, and had taken to doing even less since his retirement the previous year, sensed his moment of glory had come. Uttering a war cry garnered from kung-fu movies watched every afternoon on television and seizing a silver-headed walking stick inherited from his grandfather, he snatched away Jae's chair and threw open the door.

The first thing that happened was that his silk trousers fell down. There he was, the aging hero, dressed in a singlet and brandishing a silver-topped walking stick, with his pyjama trousers around his ankles and nothing in between, except bits of flabby flesh and patches of sparse hair. He caught sight of two young men with knives, Wanee plonked on the floor between them with a scarf tied around her mouth which was unusually immobile. Jae he could not see but sensed her behind him, humiliated by his posture.

Bight of Bangkok

The young men burst out laughing. "You silly sod. Do you think we are afraid of you?" Even in his discomfiture, Prapart realised this was not the voice of the person who had spoken before. It was slightly more educated, less rasping.

Prapart gathered up his trousers and his dignity. "What do you think you are doing in my house?" he asked imperiously.

"We've come for your money, that's what. Come on, tell us where you keep it, and stop wasting our time," Rough Voice replied.

Jae felt it was time to say something. "We don't keep money in the house. Never. And certainly not for the likes of you."

"Do yer keep it for the likes of anyone else then? Yer kids when they've not got enough to pay the instalments on the car, their kids when they want a toy the likes of us can't afford? Come off it, old girl. Don't give us crap. Give us the lolly."

Prapart made a gesture of menace. "Get out of my house!" was all he could think of to say.

"Not before we have the jewellery and the money, thanks, you old fart," said the semi-educated.

No one had ever spoken to Prapart in his life in such a way. He had no idea what to do next. His mind was made up for him. Rough Voice snatched the walking stick out of his hand and beat him on the backside with it. Smoothie tied his hands behind his back with the telephone wire, probably taken from his already useless machine. Jae tried to intervene but was quickly stopped by Rough Voice, who trussed her up too. To be sure, he tied her

Ear Off

feet together as well. She was dumped next to her second cousin on the floor.

"And now, if you please," said Smoothie, "the cash."

Prapart did not move. "The cash, please," Smoothie repeated, and lifted the knife menacingly.

Prapart remained immobile and silent. "You're asking for it, aren't you? Can't you hear or something?" Prapart was still silent. His silence irritated Smoothie more than any words might have done. "So your bloody ears are no use to you, is that it? Right, let's get rid of them, one by one!" Pulling Prapart's left ear away from his head with one hand, he brought the knife in the other down, slicing through his ear.

Prapart screamed in agony, louder than anything Wanee had produced when she met the robbers. Jae was desperate. There was no end in sight. They would all three be cut up in bits by these savages.

"Some of the money is underneath the mattress. The rest is on the bottom of the wardrobe," she said, above Prapart's howls.

"And your jewels?"

Jae hesitated. At least she knew they were insured, though only for a fraction of their value.

"Do you want his other ear to go?" Smoothie asked. Prapart moaned in pain and anguish at the thought of a repeated operation.

"In a box underneath the bed," Jae hissed.

The thieves left them to themselves. Smoothie looked under the bed and removed a jewel box, and then rummaged beneath the mattress before pulling out a small package wrapped in newspaper. Rough Voice wrenched open the wardrobe doors and dived into the bottom, coming out with a couple of large brown envelopes. They both snatched off the wrappers of their packages and looked inside with satisfaction.

"Thanks," said Smoothie. "We've had a look downstairs already. There's nothing worth having. You can keep the lot. Have a good day." They ran downstairs and disappeared.

Jae and Wanee were strung up like chickens. Prapart had only his hands tied, but was in such pain. Blood was flowing so prodigiously from what had been his ear that he was not capable of movement. Jae moved herself next to Wanee, who managed to unwind the wire strung around her mistress's wrists. Jae then freed her husband, whom she led to the bed, and Wanee was ordered to get cold water and a towel. The telephone downstairs was dead, out of order, with the wires cut as well.

They patched Prapart up as best as they could. Jae sent Wanee out of the wide-open front door into the street to get a taxi, a car, a three-wheeler, anything that moved. She found a motorbike, and sent it in search of a taxi. They were fortunate in finding one without too much delay. Jae went off with Prapart to the nearest hospital, with his detached ear placed in ice-cubes in a plastic bag. Wanee was told to phone the police and to look after the house.

The police, called from a neighbour's house, came quickly. They ascertained, when Jae and Prapart returned, that the thieves got away with some Bt.40,000 in cash.

Ear Off

The jewel box contained gold ornaments, including several chains and Buddha images, and diamonds which Jae said were worth Bt.160,000. Wanee was astounded at the value; Jae had never worn anything but tiny diamond earrings and a ring. The value of Prapart's detached ear was not decided, and the surgeons at the hospital said they were unable to restore it, and they doubted if anyone could. A nurse on duty, by way of comfort, pointed out that an ear was only decorative anyway; the hearing organs were inside the head.

The robbers were never captured. A small news item appeared in the papers with sparse details of the event, but giving the name of the street on the other side of the river where the attack took place. Many of the horrified people living nearby who read about it came around to hear the gory details and to give comfort. Prapart and Jae's two children, both married with families and homes of their own, were all for offering a reward to capture the robbers. Prapart was set against it. "What's the use? You cannot put my ear back, the money would have gone and the jewels sold." So the children bought two huge guard dogs instead and gave them to their parents. The telephone company, alerted to the trouble, for once managed to fix the phone speedily.

Prapart was all right in the end, though he had to wear for the rest of his life a bandage round what was left of his ear. Jae gave up even wearing her earrings, feeling it was too unkind a reminder to Prapart. The cash they did not really need. The robbers were right to say little downstairs was of value. But Jae sold a couple of bits of silver and some old *benjarong* bowls Prapart had inherited so that there was nothing else worth stealing. Wanee laboured on until she died of a heart attack, worn out from tending not only her master and mistress but the two dogs as well. Prapart invented a story to cover the moment of his glory, which he told endlessly to anyone who could bear to listen to him. He was himself slightly hard of hearing after the attack.

The Colonel's Lady

To be frank, she was not a lady, but she aspired to be one. She wanted so much for her husband to get promoted and become a general; it was only a question of time, of course, she knew that. Then, with luck (or so she thought), it would be more or less automatic, she would get a decoration and be able to style herself *khunying*, like other generals' wives. Who knows, if things turned out well, if good fortune came her husband's way, if she did lots of charity work, she might even become a *thanpuying*. But she decided that modesty should prevail, at least for the present. *Khunying* would be enough.

She came from an ordinary family of petty traders in Pitsanuloke, half-Chinese of course, and had gone to secondary school there. It was there she had met her future husband, Saiyud, then a young officer cadet. He was dashing, smart, well-turned out. Not much of a ladies' man, and certainly not the possessor of a brilliant mind. But he had a future. She could see that. He would rise through the ranks and she would too.

Saiyud courted Montana as he should. Her parents were pleased. One less daughter to worry about if it came off. And he had an assured future. No one quit the army, it was a job for life, with all sorts of business opportunities along the way, and a welcome pension at the end. There was no war around, which is why the borders were only lightly defended, and no enemies, so the army could safely gather most of its forces close to the capital and keep an eye on affairs of the state.

They married, had three children. The boy was naturally destined for the army, and because of his father had easy access to the right schools and later to a good position in the junior officer ranks. He was dim, but that did not matter. The brawn counted. The two girls, Montana herself had to admit, were something of a disaster. Neither pretty nor gracious, neither bright nor talented, she really did not know what to do with them. They spent most of the day dressing up and the weekends walking around shopping centres in the capital.

Saiyud and Montana did not have to stay long in the provincial outpost of Pitsanuloke. No sir, Saiyud got a post which involved cushy office hours in the secretariat in Rajadamnern. They bought a car, and some land on the Thonburi side. They built a rather fancy house on it. They did not have to worry too much about money. Montana asked no questions, and was given enough to keep her happy. She invested not only in chit funds but also, more sensibly, in jewels. She was not prepared to be an impoverished first wife if Saiyud took a mistress, or a minor wife in the local parlance. What he did in his spare time was his affair, as far as she was concerned. He started to play golf, not that he really liked the game, but it gave him the excuse to get out of his office, and he met the right people on the tees. Montana was pretty sure he was having it off with one of the women caddies at one stage, but she decided to say nothing, and simply increased her expenditure on jewels.

She allowed herself to run to fat. She enjoyed her food, she took no exercise, she had a maid to do most of the work. She spent hours in the hairdresser's, who worked up her naturally limp hair into a vast beehive at least three times a week. There she listlessly turned over the pages of women's magazines, without a thought passing through her head.

To her peers, she was as sweet as could be. But she developed snobbery to a fine art, and looked down her nose on junior officers' wives, getting her own back for the snubs she had formerly endured. She became, in short, a bitch. As Saiyud rose in rank, she was able to dispense with the maid, for the army provided two privates doing their military service. She treated them like dirt.

"You little twerps, you hogs, don't you know how to clean properly? Get down on your knees and do the floors again." She released all her frustrations on these poor creatures, who came from the north-east and thought they would be able to learn a trade if they joined the army. The only trade they learnt was how to clean Montana's house. A slave-driver in ancient Rome would have shown more consideration to the two than Montana.

They shared a single servant's room with a leaky roof, and when quite sure they were on their own, plotted their revenge.

"I'll poke her eyes out with a skewer, the old cow," said Kasem.

"That's too good for her. Roast her alive, so her screams will be heard in hell," replied his mate, Chalong.

They fantasised endlessly, and began to fail to realise they were entering an unreal world where their only object was to get even with the beehived tyrant. They were both ordinary enough boys who had selected red balls when they were twenty-one years old and the time came for the annual recruitment exercise in the local district. Though they both came from Chaturat, they were from different villages, and they had not known each other before fate threw them together in their Pranburi camp. However, they did not stay there long, for they were soon detailed to Bangkok as unpaid servants (unpaid at least by Montana, though paid a pittance by the state).

When Kao Pansar, the beginning of the Buddhist Lent, came up in July, Chalong asked for permission to go home for two days, which were government holidays. "My elder brother is entering the monkhood, and I would like to attend the ceremony and help at home."

"Home?" snarled Montana. "You don't come from a home. You come from a sty. You are certainly not going home. You're here to work for me, and in the army, orders are orders. You obey me."

The young men talked it over between themselves. There was nothing they could do. But Chalong decided to go anyway. He sneaked out and took the bus back home.

Montana was beside herself with fury. She said nothing to Saiyud, who would have fairly pointed out that the boys had the right to be on leave for two days. She made life even more unbearable for Kasem. He had five hours' sleep for the two days Chalong was absent. And when Chalong returned, she was burning with rage.

"You disobeyed my orders," she said. "I forbade you to go away. I shall have Colonel Saiyud put you in the military jail in Pranburi. For the rest of your days. You deserve that, you pig. Wanted to go back to your sty, did you? I'll give you what you asked for." She made as if to strike him with a crystal vase on the table.

She had gone too far. Chalong's temper was roused, and Kasem, who was witness to the scene, came to defend his pal.

"Put that down, you old bag," Chalong told her, "otherwise you'll get what you deserve."

"Me? Me get what I deserve? It's you who will get what you deserve. Jail, with hard labour."

The rest was unpremeditated. No one else was in the house. Colonel Saiyud was probably on the golf course, the girls wandering around a shopping centre buying clothes they did not need, and the boy was in camp. Chalong snatched a heavy ash tray on the table and brought it down smartly on her head. She screamed for help, uselessly.

Kasem joined in. "Take that, take that," he said as he pierced her with a bread knife. Chalong had taken the pestle from the kitchen and was beating her brains out with it. The mess on the floor was indescribable.

"Just look at your nice floor now, you whore," he said.

They dragged the body into the toilet and stuck the

head into the bowl. For good measure the pestle was placed over it. Perhaps they thought devils could return to the bodies they had left.

"What are we going to do now?" Kasem asked. "We'll be shot."

"If they catch us. Come, we'll take the old bitch's car. Go and get her jewels, you know where they are. I can drive. We must get out of here as fast as we can."

They took as much money as they could find; there was not much. But they also took her credit cards, and as much of the jewellery as they could without it seeming too obvious. Closing the door of the house carefully after them and locking the windows just out of habit, they drove off.

They did not get very far, because the car ran out of petrol. They decided it was too risky to be seen with the car anyway.

"We mustn't go home. That's the first place they will look for us. Better to go where we are not known."

They made their way down to Chumporn, where they managed to get hired by a fishing boat that illegally fished in Malaysian waters. It was risky, but the profits were good. They were sensible enough not to try to sell any of the jewels.

The manhunt for them went on for months, but like the drivers involved in serious traffic accidents, they "had fled the scene." Their families never heard from them again. Some say they became involved in a fight with pirates in the Gulf, others say that they became pirates themselves. Saiyud became a general, and his minor wife was elevated in rank to first wife, and then after a time became a *khunying*. But she was sweetness itself and genuinely concerned about those less fortunate than her; after all, she had known what it was like to work as a caddie and earn one's living.

The Consul's Daughter

Keiko was an attractive girl, about 15 years old perhaps less, pale, with beautiful eyes, slender legs, and was clearly intelligent. She started going to the activities of the Thai cultural club of Silapakorn University in order, she said, to get to know more about the country she was living in. She spoke little Thai and less English, but was happy to speak in Japanese with anyone else who was proficient in the language. Unfortunately few were, but usually she managed to find at least one person with whom to communicate after a fashion.

She did not attend the lectures that were organised, of course, but went along to the film and slide shows that were arranged, and showed particular interest in architecture.

At a meeting in Silapakorn she got into conversation with someone who had a rather broken knowledge of her language.

"Where do you come from?" he asked.

"From Osaka. Or at least my father does. But we have lived many years abroad."

"Where did you go?"

"Oh, several countries in Africa, to Brazil, but this is

our first time in South-East Asia."

"What does your father do?" came the question.

"He's the consul here," she replied, modestly. "He signs visas and things."

Her interlocutor translated this into Thai to the others nearby, who at once became more deferential towards the girl, not just because of her family connection, but because it might be necessary to have use of that connection at some stage: visas to Japan were increasingly hard to obtain.

The Silapakorn club arranged trips to the provinces which Keiko was very keen to join.

"My father wants me to see as much of the country as possible," she said, "but does not like the idea of me going around on my own. So I'm sure it will be all right if I go with you." She produced a document in Japanese, which was beyond the capacity of anyone to read, apparently asking those concerned to take care of her. She was assured that everything would be all right.

The forthcoming journey organised by the club was tabled to visit palaces and temples in Petchaburi: the palace of King Vajiravudh at Nakorn Pathom, which now serves the provincial administration, was to be seen on the way, the Khao Luang palace of King Mongkut in the middle of Petchaburi itself, Wat Yai Suwannaram, and several other interesting temples in the town. After that, they were to go on to Cha-am, where they would stay overnight at a hotel, relax the following morning, see the great teak palace of King Vajiravudh by the sea there, and then return.

Bight of Bangkok

The trip took place the following week. Thanks to advance notice being given of Keiko's presence, the Silapakorn bus was given a police escort all the way, flashing lights to clear a path through the dense traffic. They reached Nakorn Pathom in no time, and officials laid on delicious snacks and provided a local interpreter for Keiko while there. Off then to Petchaburi itself, where again the provincial authorities really put themselves out, and provided an excellent lunch for the entire group after they had come down from admiring the restored palace at the top of the hill.

Keiko expressed much pleasure at being able to see the temples. "Our Buddhist temples in Japan are so different from yours, though of course we use a lot of wood as well in their construction."

"*So-odeska,*" said the only person with a passing knowledge of Japanese in the group.

The police escort whisked them off after visiting Petchaburi to Cha-am, where the hotel they were booked in went overboard. The manager, in a dark formal suit and a bow tie, greeted Keiko and other members of the group. A welcome fruit punch was served, they showered and changed, and then the district officer and a small party came to take Keiko and the leader of the group, Acharn Sombat, out to a lavish dinner in another hotel.

One man in the party had lived in Japan a couple of years, and tried to engage Keiko in conversation, but she was rather shy, possibly because she thought he was trying to get off with her, and kept her distance, limiting the conversation to banalities. She was, after all, rather young.

The Consul's Daughter

The group returned the next day as planned, greatly enjoying the perfect site of the palace inside the army compound at what is called Fort Vajiravudh (though the compound came later), and then returned without incident to Bangkok. Entry into the capital, normally a nightmare, was made easy, thanks to the police escort.

The group disbanded inside the courtyard of the university, and the consul's daughter expressed her gratitude for all that had been done to make the journey so pleasant and memorable. She was offered a lift home but politely refused, saying everyone was tired and needed a rest. Acharn Sombat, who spoke no Japanese at all, offered to take her to Sukhumwit (he guessed she lived there, like all Japanese), but she firmly declined his offer, and gracefully made her exit, presumably to catch a taxi. He did not see her off as he had a number of small details to attend to at the end of the trip. All agreed it was very successful.

Sombat was rather puzzled when he saw her a couple of days later in the university. There was no cultural event taking place, and Keiko did not appear to have any purpose in being there. "Perhaps she arranged to meet someone on the trip here," he thought. But then he realised that was impossible, since no one in the group spoke Japanese.

He considered the matter a while and then looked in the telephone directory. Few people in Bangkok normally do this, because most names were not in it and the numbers changed so frequently that it was out of date before it was even published. But he guessed the number he was looking for was not likely to have changed too often. He dialled the number he wanted.

"Is that the Japanese Embassy?"

"Yes. What can we do for you?"

Acharn Sombat asked for the consul. "I am afraid he's very busy now. Could you tell me what is this about?" Sombat politely explained, saying he was asking for confirmation that the consul indeed had a daughter named Keiko who was following outside lectures in Thai culture.

The telephone operator said, "I'll give you the consul's secretary."

The secretary was efficient and to the point. "No, I'm afraid the consul has no daughter. There is a young girl who is often hanging about the embassy, and we have heard from other sources that this girl claims she is related to embassy staff. But I'm afraid she is no more than a vagrant."

"And she is not Japanese?"

"Not as far as we know."

"I see. Thank you."

He thought for a minute after putting down the phone. What course of action should he take? Call in the police? He had no grounds to do so, and it would make him and the university, not to speak of all the provincial officials, look foolish.

He called in another teacher, Acharn Aroon, who had also been on the trip, and told him what he had discovered. Aroon was astonished they could have been taken in so easily. They went in search of the girl but there was no sign of her. They agreed to call her in when they next saw her, that is if she came near the university again, and question her.

The opportunity was not long in coming. The cultural club was holding a traditional Thai music occasion at the end of the week, and sure enough "Keiko" came along. Before anything started, Acharn Sombat and Aroon firmly escorted her to Sombat's office nearby.

Speaking in Thai, Sombat said, "I know you are not Japanese. I was in touch with the embassy. Tell me who you really are!"

"Keiko" tried some more Japanese, then some English. "I am a Lao princess escaping from the bad men in my country."

"Tell the truth," said Aroon, in Thai. "You're Thai, aren't you? Where do you come from?"

Seeing the game was up, "Keiko" nodded, and said "Chiangsaen, in Chiangrai province."

"And why did you pretend you were the daughter of a Japanese diplomat?"

"Because I thought I would be well treated."

In that, Sombat mused, she was right.

"And where did you learn Japanese?"

"I went to a number of Japanese language schools, and studied hard. Eventually I thought I could get to Japan, if I found someone to help me."

"Why did you leave your home? Why do you want to go to Japan?" asked Sombat, though he could have answered the questions himself; she presumably left home because there was no money, and wanted to go to Japan to make some.

Bight of Bangkok

At first she did not answer, and then replied to only the second question. "I wanted to marry someone who would look after me."

"And why did you leave Chiangsaen?" persisted Aroon.

"My parents wanted to sell me into a brothel."

"How old are you?" asked Sombat, fatherly, feeling sorry for the girl.

"Thirteen. My parents are peasants and have no money."

By this time both the lecturers had forgotten all about the cultural event taking place, though the music of the xylophones, metallophones and the flute could be heard in the background.

"What level at school did you finish?"

"The sixth class of primary school. There was no money to continue."

The lecturers were amazed. This young girl had succeeded in fooling them all, and they thought she was well educated; instead, she had barely finished primary school. Inwardly, Sombat grudgingly admired her; he was reminded of a film he had seen long ago, *My Fair Lady*. But the girl in the film had an English professor to teach her. This girl had had no one, and she had taught herself Japanese; he could barely communicate in English, the most common foreign language, and which he had studied for years to little purpose.

"How have you managed to live in Bangkok?"

"As best I could." They knew what that probably meant.

"We shall have to hand you over to the authorities. You cannot live on the streets like this."

"I don't mind staying in a home, if I can learn something.

The Consul's Daughter

But please, please don't send me back home to Chiangsaen; I would rather die."

"Don't worry, they won't do that." He telephoned the Nang Lerng police station and explained the case, saying he was bringing the girl around immediately.

The station was sympathetic. They allowed her to stay there until the Juvenile and Youth Welfare Division could arrange to place her in a home. A real home, from where she would not be sold.

Child Divine

In the mid-1980s, the Thai newspapers were, for almost a month, full of the story of the divine doctor, an inspired child said to be capable of curing all sorts of illnesses.

Panja Kerdnawk was his parents' fifth child. His father explained how he was special to a reporter. "One day while playing near the village pond, our Lek fell into it. He was too young to swim and drowned. But after an hour, he came to the surface again, still alive, and holding a piece of root in his hand. As he emerged from the water, our son told us that he was a god who had been born again to make people well. Then he gave his mother the piece of root which he was holding, telling her to take it as it would cure her. My wife had been sick for many years with a wasting disease so she boiled the root in water and drank the brew. She got better, almost at once."

At his early curing sessions, the three-year-old boy would sit before great numbers of water bowls, each with a one baht coin at the bottom. Next to the bowls was a pile of roots, said to have medicinal value, collected by his family from the nearby forest. He would murmur as if chanting, wreathing himself in smoke from a cigarette

Child Divine

in his hand; his patients and curious onlookers watched spellbound. He would then stand up and walk or, more often, was carried around in a circle. His patients would follow, picking up the roots and putting them into their bowls along the way. After following in the circle three times or more, they would turn their bowls over, depositing the coins in front of the boy's house. The sessions ended in this way, and the roots were then taken away for use in curing sickness or offering to others.

The god child showed great maturity and wisdom. At a very early stage he had declared, through his parents, that every coin received from those who sought his help must be deposited in the bank. The branch manager at Chaturat supported this divine prudence.

His reputation grew amazingly. At first, people from nearby villages came to Baan Yaa Kaa in Chaturat district in the province of Chaiyapoom. This is in the poor northeast, where villagers were ready to believe in short-cuts to health as well as wealth, on earth or in heaven. Gradually the cult extended, first throughout his province, then through the whole region. The rich came in cars, the majority in chartered buses; those living nearby came on bicycles or in bullock carts.

Within a couple of weeks the crowds were vast and the authorities became concerned. The police feared they could no longer keep order, the health authorities worried that this curious form of alternative medicine would lead to people abandoning both western and traditional medicine. Social workers said the boy was suffering from malnutrition and exhaustion. As the numbers swelled, civil servants in the Department of Public Welfare became concerned that a small group was using Panja in a giant confidence trick.

Local entrepreneurs, who were raking in money for all they were worth, did not share the worries of officialdom. They charged 20 baht a day for stands to the vendors who came from nearby villages and even the town to sell fried chicken, coconut pasties, papaya and chilli salad, toasted meat balls, home-prepared noodles, fried bananas, fruits, soft (and, with discretion, hard) drinks. Ten baht a day was charged for parking irrespective of whether it was for a bus or car, and every open space became a parking lot. Holes were dug in the ground and screened by corrugated iron; for the use of these toilets one paid two baht a time.

Maw Lek, the 'little doctor', did not appear to profit by the commotion himself, but no doubt his family did. According to the police, they were earning at least 20,000 baht a day, more than double what most earned traditionally after a year of toil. A businessman from the provincial capital entered into negotiations with the village headman to set up a special parking lot, two hundred stands for vendors, and superior lavatories, promising the village a share of the profits.

The crowds grew bigger by the day, and Dr Lek more exhausted. He had to be carried around the village on the shoulders of his assistants, who were mostly relatives. He was sometimes crying, and his eyes were puffed from lack of sleep. The police threatened to charge his father, Pradit Kerdnawk, and his accomplices with cheating. If that would not stick they would try illegal logging, a catch-all charge, which the gathering of a few roots might at a pinch cover.

The provincial authorities repeatedly warned the public that the herbs provided by the little doctor, whom they less charitably called a quack, were ineffective. It had no effect. Three weeks after the miracles started, ten thousand people were coming each day to the village, all suffering from a variety of illnesses, most of which could be put down to poverty and poor food.

The local authorities being unable to cope, the national ones were called in. The appropriate ministry issued a statement:

> *The Ministry wishes to make clear that the treatment of the child known as Doctor Lek is useless and the so-called herbs he prescribes have never been recognised even by traditional doctors.*

The pronouncement continued:

> *People who have sought treatment from the quack might feel their condition to be improved, whereas there had been no healing whatever.*

The Deputy Permanent Secretary of the Ministry — no less — spoke publicly, "On the subject of the child known as Doctor Lek, I should point out that the condition of the patients might deteriorate if they forsook proper treatment for superstition." He added, "I feel it my duty to say that the health of the so-called doctor himself has deteriorated through overwork and undernourishment."

Bight of Bangkok

After four weeks of increasing crowds and chaos, the authorities decided to act and not to rely on empty threats. They put up five roadblocks leading to Baan Yaa Kaa, and the police superintendent, with the exalted rank of lieutenant-colonel, negotiated with Doctor Lek's parents, who agreed to make the last treatment session on that day. The superintendent quite rightly said the boy looked unwell and in need of a rest.

A month before, the crowds had only numbered a few hundreds, but newspaper and television reports had ensured success, and some fifty thousand a day were coming to be cured by the boy. People in chartered buses from all over the north-east, the north and even from Bangkok were coming daily. Once at the village each visitor had to pay ten baht for a plastic bowl containing a candle, joss sticks, and two cigarettes as a donation to the child divine. They placed one baht in the bowl as an offering. The crowds were vast, squatting on the ground in the sun, roped off behind massed rows, five deep on either side, of plastic bowls each containing offerings. They ate their sticky rice from woven containers and waited patiently, as they had done for all their lives, for some good to come their way. Doctor Lek was carried on the shoulders of his assistants who made a triumphant procession past the plastic bowls. The child raised his hands in gestures resembling blessings, and occasionally puffed at some of the offerings received; smoking was a common enough practice among very young boys in the north-east.

In spite of the roadblocks and police warnings, many villagers on that last day walked five kilometres to the village. One group verbally attacked the police and came close to blows. "The boy is curing poor people's sicknesses for one baht. That's cheaper than any of your fancy government doctors."

"You shouldn't stop his assistants from collecting bark and herbs. Everyone can go into the forest reserve. He's not causing any damage." The police had their orders, and pointed out that with fifty thousand people a day coming, the forest was being stripped bare.

Another group in Dr Lek's defence told the local officials, "You know, the prime minister is coming soon to call on the little doctor."

"And the supreme commander of the armed forces as well," chimed in one of this group, with claimed access to privileged information.

Dr Lek's patrons organised a small demonstration in front of the police station at Chaturat, the village being much too small to boast such an amenity.

His last appearance was splendid. Borne aloft by a cousin, his tiny arms holding onto the young man's head and his thin legs dangling from his shoulders, Dr Lek leaned forward, his lips pursed, his eyes squinting in the sun. Lined on either side of a rope marking out the processional path were thousands of patients. Plastic bowls, each with a couple of roots and a stick of wood, were massed all along the route. People dressed in their best, some holding umbrellas for protection against the scorching sun, squatted on the ground waiting for him to pass. As he did so, they raised their hands in a gesture of respect and bowed their heads, as they would before a revered monk. The crowd was by then far too large for everyone to pass in front of the boy's house to deposit their baht offering. Instead, four assistants followed the little doctor, each with a plastic sack, into which people dropped their coins. As the sacks filled the assistants carried them off and replaced them with fresh ones.

When Dr Lek had completed his peregrination, he simply puffed once at a cigarette offered to him by his bearer, bowed his head, and slid off his shoulders to the ground. His father and mother, on either side, escorted him back to their house where he promptly fell asleep. The crowds slowly dispersed, each clasping their roots and stick.

His parents kept their word. There were no more appearances, in spite of appeals from Dr Lek's followers. The village of Baan Yaa Kaa gradually returned to its wonted calm, though the mess created by the parking lots and the toilets took a long time to clear up. The local bank manager was pleased that there were no more sacks of coins to count, but regretted the decline in business after all was over. The entrepreneur was furious at the police intervention but consoled himself by planning to develop a similar scheme at a recently restored old temple site in the region.

And Dr Lek and his parents? They remained quietly in the village, and did not remove, as many had predicted. They bought a 24-inch colour television set and then built an indoor toilet with a cement floor, which the villagers thought very luxurious. A small team of reporters returned to the village a couple of years later and interviewed the boy before he started school. He seemed ordinary enough. He took them through the thin woods and, with rather vague gestures, pointed out which trees and shrubs provided roots, leaves, bark and twigs that, according to him, could cure people. Whether he was right or was misleading them they did not know. He appeared to believe himself what he was saying. His family might not have forgotten the momentous happenings of the past, but was clearly unwilling to talk about them. They certainly did not treat Panja like a god any more. This now ordinary mortal still enjoyed smoking. When asked what he would like to become when he finished school, his answer was firm: "A policeman."

Miss Plastic Rose

Mongkol had met Kim one Saturday night at Hua Lampang, the main railway station in Bangkok. Both were lonely. Mongkol had come to Bangkok some months before from the northern province of Lampang. There was no work in his village, except as a farmer, but his family had insufficient land and too many mouths to feed. But he enjoyed being with the boys in his village, and managed to satisfy them without anyone worrying too much. Everyone knew him and accepted him without question.

"He's just like a girl," his grandmother would say, acknowledging the fact of life without any concern. "He prefers the company of boys."

There was someone like him in nearly every village. With his painted fingernails, his long curly hair loose, he waggled his slim hips in the evening as he walked down to the river to bathe with the other young men. They joked with him and some laughed at him, but still, they came to him for the services he provided. He did not charge, and everyone was happy. It was not that the girls were closely chaperoned, but simply that they knew how to hold out better than the boys for what they wanted, which was usually a firm offer of marriage, and the boys were indifferent to the forms their pleasure took.

Mongkol, barely fifteen, had come to Bangkok out of financial rather than emotional need, but found the capital equally poor in satisfying either. It was terribly difficult to find a job, and he drifted through several dead-end daily-hired positions. He had no qualifications, other than a pleasing nature, a ready smile like most of his compatriots, and vestigial learning provided by one of the less well-endowed state primary schools in his village.

He made money as best as he could, often by what he politely referred to as his "evening work" which was uncertain, but fairly early on in his stay, a stroke of luck came his way. His evening occupations put him in contact with the rather portly owner of a unisex hairdressing saloon. Sensing Mongkol might have some flair, he asked, "Would you like to learn to cut people's hair? I might be able to help you."

"I'd love to. It's something I've dreamed about," he said truthfully.

So he was taken on, and became very good at it in a remarkably short time. The boss lived his own life, with many different unisex liaisons, and left Mongkol to his own devices. He became a relatively skilled hairdresser, but his life was empty.

He had, by accident, found a room to live in quite early on in his stay. The owner of the building was a Chinese who was probably engaged in a number of other businesses, of greater or lesser legality, in addition to renting out rooms in a house located not far from the station. For those who actually found work and did not have to sleep in the square in front of the station, like so many from the provinces, Ah Seng's modest lodgings provided shelter of a kind: a tiny room with nothing in it except a single light bulb, well-covered with fly dirt and its flex wreathed in cobwebs, and a bathroom of sorts with a squat toilet shared by numerous other tenants.

There Mongkol installed himself with a sleeping mat, a pillow, a collapsible plastic wardrobe, a broken mirror and a couple of pails in which he did his washing. He ate out from any one of the many food stalls or vendors in the locality. He was well-off compared to many.

It was here that he discreetly entertained his friends on occasions, when they did not provide the luxury of a hotel with a soft bed and sheets which seemed to make life so much more comfortable. But he was cautious of getting on the wrong side of Ah Seng for he might need his support. Ah Seng could not care less what any of his lodgers did so long as they kept quiet and paid their rent on time; if they were even half a day late in paying their dues, though, he was merciless.

One Saturday night, friendless, Mongkol wandered into the station. He saw the foreign hippies with their pony tails, filthy jeans and bedraggled shirts looking at his painted nails and made-up eyes with distaste as they hauled their backpacks into the evening trains going to places Mongkol could not afford to visit.

He looked with increasing desperation at possible companions for the night and then saw Kim. His well-built frame made Mongkol envious. He began a somewhat

Miss Plastic Rose

inane conversation with Kim.

"Where do you come from?" Mongkol asked.

"Korat. And you?"

"Lampang," Mongkol replied. "Are you married?"

"Yes, but I don't see my wife often. Can't afford the fare."

"Where do you stay?"

The north-easterner replied, "Wherever I can. I move around, depending on what work I can find. Do you live near here?" he asked.

"Yes, just around the corner. Are you doing anything now?" Mongkol asked.

"No, I'm free."

"Would you like to come to my place?" asked Mongkol.

Kim knew perfectly well what he was being asked for. "Fine, let's go." He had nothing else to do and nowhere to go. Mongkol was lucky he was not picked up by one of the vice squad for prostituting himself in a public place. Fortune was to smile on him more than once in his life.

Kim came and enjoyed himself. Both of them had missed real human warmth for so long. Kim returned the following evening uninvited, when Mongkol was about to go out and look for him. Soon, they drifted into cohabitation. Mongkol gave Kim all that he could and ceased to take on "special clients". He shared what he earned with Kim, but the relationship was unequal. Kim's employment as a coolie in the harbour was much more uncertain than Mongkol's, and when he did have money he tried to send some home to support his wife and many children. Mongkol's relative youth and basically passive nature allowed Kim to start bossing him around; arguments over money began. Mongkol, to make ends meet, tried to earn extra from night clients and the relationship soured. It ended with a violent argument with Kim demanding a bottle of Mekong, for which he had no money for. He stormed out of their room on being told he could not have it. Ah Seng, reading a paper downstairs, raised a disapproving eyebrow at the noise of his departure but otherwise was unconcerned; it was the beginning of the month and the rent had been paid in advance.

Kim felt the relationship had to come to an end; here he was, a married man, but virtually married to another. He could go home to his wife. But that would solve nothing. He had no money and was tired of asking Mongkol for some.

"There is only one way out," he thought. "I must get arrested. In jail I can escape Mongkol and also get fed."

But how could he get arrested? "You have to steal something," Kim thought to himself. He snatched a gold necklace from the first person who passed, an ugly young woman with a squint. She squinted even more when she saw Kim just standing there by a power pole, necklace in hand, and not attempting to run away.

"Are you crazy?" she asked, really thinking he must be.

"No. I just want to get arrested." She decided he was totally mad, found a policeman nearby, and explained what had happened. "I think he's a nut case. Ought to be locked up. But in a hospital, not a prison."

At this point, Mongkol, wearing high heels and a dress,

Miss Plastic Rose

appeared on the scene which was very close to Ah Seng's establishment. He saw Kim, very meekly being led away by the policeman with the girl with the squint following. He rushed up.

"Please don't send him to jail. We have been living together for some time, but have had a silly quarrel. Kim only took the necklace to go to jail, and wanted to end our affair." The word 'affair' came out without him really wanting it to.

"No go," said the policeman, thinking they really were a rather odd couple.

"Then take me to jail as well," pleaded Mongkol.

"It's not a hotel, you know. No." The policeman marched Kim off to the nearest station to book him. Kim made no attempt to resist.

Mongkol hated the prospect of living alone again. His only thought was to be with Kim. And the only way he could be was to be put in jail as well. These thoughts passed rapidly through his mind and he wandered down the street and turned into another. But of course, it was obvious, he must commit a crime too.

Like Kim, Mongkol stole a gold necklace, went through the same motions as Kim, was arrested with pleasure, and taken to a police station. But Kim was not there. A policeman on duty explained that Mongkol had snatched the necklace in one district, and where his friend was arrested was in another. The jail would be different. Mongkol broke down and wept.

By local standards, his trial was a remarkably swift and simple affair. Mongkol admitted guilt and, because of his youth and having no previous conviction of any kind, was sentenced to one year of occupational training in a remand home for girls, since that was how he was dressed.

No doubt the judge thought he was doing Mongkol a service; after all, he would not be at the mercy of other boys and could learn another skill. So off he went to Ban Kredtrakaan in Nonthaburi. This home provided training courses in domestic arts, sewing and the like to female prostitutes, who occupied the home in diminishing numbers. Far from being in short supply, the authorities were overwhelmed by the scale of their activities, and simply gave up arresting and prosecuting them. Mongkol was the only male among some two hundred women who were all there under duress and most were longing to return to their former occupation, which paid so much better than anything more respectable they were likely to earn, given their lack of education and accomplishments.

Training in the remand home suited Mongkol fine; even the guardian, Khun Wanida, had to admit that Mongkol's behaviour was a model to all, and he diligently followed courses in shirt-making, fruit-cutting, and laying tables, because he was genuinely interested in such things. His mother had never taught him anything like that; they did not even have a table in his home.

However, the women there made life hell for Mongkol. He tried to help them, by doing their hair up nicely and trying different styles. But they were starving, ravenous for men. And there were nearly two hundred of them. They were quite shameless. When the supervisors were not looking, they stripped him of his clothes, they grabbed his privates, they held him down naked on the floor and tried to obtain satisfaction from him. Mongkol, by his nature was totally unable to satisfy even one of them, much less two hundred. Still further frustrated, dying of thirst besides the fountain as the French poet had it, they became furious, tearing at his hair, pinching and punching him. "We want a man, a man, a man," they shrieked in a wild chorus. "And all we get is you! Take that, and that," they cried as they hit him until his screams brought the guards to his rescue.

Always slightly withdrawn, Mongkol became neurotic. He ran away when one of the other inmates came near him, and locked himself in the lavatory. It took all the assurances and pleadings of several guards to coax him out of his retreat. They took pity on him and locked him up by himself in a room at night. He asked to be taken to a prison like other men. They suspected his motives: "Sorry, you have to stay here for the full year," was the official reply.

That year became purgatory for Mongkol. One night there was a staff party in another part of the building. Several other inmates crowded outside his locked door. One had managed to get a duplicate of the key and unlocked it. Mongkol ran out of the room, trying to escape from them. They rushed after him. In desperation, he jumped through a ground floor window, badly twisting his ankle in the process, and sought shelter in the staff building.

The lady director of the establishment decided this could not go on; he was blameless, it was the other girls who caused trouble. Mongkol was admitted to a male prison hospital, where, after his ankle was better and he could walk properly again, he stayed to finish the final weeks of his sentence, helping in the various hospital chores and really making himself most useful. He was essentially a home bird.

The ward superintendent, who had taken an interest in him, asked him what he was going to do when he left. He knew about Kim; the story had appeared in the papers. "Will you see Kim again?" he asked.

"No. That's all over. But I want to have someone to love me. I want a man."

"What can you do?"

Mongkol told him about his hairdressing skills. "You should go back to that. You could make extra money by working in a bar at night, but you must be careful, you know. Take precautions."

"That's an idea. Maybe I'll find the right person that way," Mongkol replied.

With his developing maturity and quite attractive looks, and after several attempts, he managed to obtain work serving in a transvestite bar in the evenings. His former hairdressing connections helped, and he was also able to continue that trade in the day. He greatly admired some of the others working with him at night. They initiated him into their little secrets, how the right hormones helped develop the bosom, the right kind of face powder to use, what brand of girdles emphasised the hips to the best effect. The bar owner, a kindly madam, warned him, "This kind of thing is all right. But don't go in for the big

Miss Plastic Rose

snip. Many regret it, you know."

"But how can I find someone who will love me and look after me for what I am?" Mongkol asked.

"There are plenty around who will," the worldy-wise lady replied.

She was right. After working some five years, and being careful with money, Mongkol managed to set aside some savings. He followed a course at a beauty school and even enrolled in Sukhothai Dhammathiraj Open University. Some talent scouts appeared one night in the bar and noticed him. By now he had grown into a most attractive young woman — tall, well-shaped, long flowing hair, wore a charming smile, with even a certain amount of sophistication.

"Hey, dearie, how about joining our competition?"

"What competition?"

"Why, the 'Miss Plastic Rose' show!" Mongkol knew something about that. There was a pageant every year in Nakorn Sawan, and the most beautiful transvestite was chosen and crowned. "I'm not pretty enough," Mongkol replied modestly.

"Yes, you are. Now, what's your name? Mongkol? That won't do. You need a nice feminine stage name. How about Sarapee?"

Mongkol shook his head. He had an aunt called Sarapee.

"Wipawadee?" Mongkol agreed to that.

The bar owner willingly agreed to Mongkol's absence to take part in the pageant. This would bring fame and trade to her establishment. 'Wipawadee' went up to the provincial city with one of her sponsors, was given a woman's swimming costume, bought a magnificent white dress, had her hair done beautifully, and practised walking up and down the catwalk, along with many others. Mongkol thought he had little chance. His sponsor was not so gloomy.

"You've got what it takes, you know. Give it to them."

Mongkol did, on the night. There was a huge crowd gathered in the provincial hall for the event. Television cameras from Bangkok were there. The razzmatazz was incredible. Mongkol was very excited by it all. The selection committee, which included the district head and various other worthies, watched carefully, and kept the scores under different headings — looks, poise, modesty and so on. Rather like a boxing match in reverse.

The chairman of the committee, after the parade of the final thirty-eight short-listed contestants was over and the judges had conferred at length, went up to the microphone, cleared his throat, and said, "We are pleased to announce that the winner is Wipawadee from Lampang. Second prize to Nirucha from Nakorn Srithammaraj. And third prize to Phailin from Mukdahan. I would like to invite the queen of the evening to come up and accept the crown." Obviously the committee had decided to distribute the prizes fairly among the regions.

Mongkol was too pleased to blush. Stepping carefully onto the platform in his sequined satin dress (on which much of his savings had been expended), he curtseyed before the chief judge, who placed a tinsel crown on his head, and gave him a gigantic plastic rose and a cup of the sporting trophy type to hold.

Miss Plastic Rose

"I declare you the winner of the competition Miss Plastic Rose for this year."

The applause was tumultuous. Immediately Mongkol was surrounded by reporters, asking him what he wanted in life, what his hopes were. Flashlights popped, cameras zoomed in. It was a great occasion.

"Now, we'd like you to tell the world," — the questioner was a little pompous — "to tell the whole world what your long-term plans are."

Mongkol did not hesitate. "Find a man I like. And also have a sex change and become a woman. I want to marry."

The questioner said something suitably daft for his audience. "There, listeners, Miss Plastic Rose for the year has one ambition, two maybe" — he could count — "to find a man and change her sex. But she's great as she is, isn't she?" he asked somewhat rhetorically to those around, and presumably his unseen audience.

Various shouts of appreciation. "Wipee, we like you as you are, darling. No funny business."

Another piped up, "These operations are expensive and difficult, you know. And not always successful."

The reporter came back to the charge. "So that's your long-term plan, young lady. How about the short-term?" He made Mongkol's proposed life sound like something put together by the United Nations or mapped out on a bank planning sheet.

"Yes, please tell us what you are going to do now you have the prize," asked another.

"Well, I have to go back to Lampang next week, because

Bight of Bangkok

I am twenty-one and have to go for selection for national service."

The reporters could not believe their luck. What a photo-opportunity as Miss Plastic Rose bared his now well-developed bosom before the crowd!

The following week, the crowd in Lampang was almost as large as that at Nakorn Sawan for the competition. Fortunately the army was alerted in advance. National security was at stake.

"Bad for discipline, to have one like that in the ranks," muttered one tough sergeant with a pineapple-pocked face.

"She'll keep the boys happy. Maybe others too."

"Yes, but it's not on. They'd be late and worn out for parade each morning."

It was not on. For Wipawadee appeared in a one-piece dress, with a thin belt showing her slender waist at its best, and was much too shy to take her dress off before the assembled reporters. She might have the right height, the requisite weight, but she did not have, the board agreed, the qualities needed of a soldier. She was not even given the chance to pick a ball out of a priest's begging bowl to decide her fate.

When Mongkol heard he was not to be recruited, he kissed the sergeant on the cheek.

More impromptu press interviews. Lampang had never seen anything like it. "And now what will you do?" was the most persistent question.

"I shall try to marry a foreigner. I want someone to love me all my life."

Miss Plastic Rose

Did she? Well, not at once. She went back to work in the bar in Bangkok. She deferred her sex change, for she married an Italian tourist who curiously failed to notice, or, having noticed, was unconcerned, that she was a he.

It does indeed take all sorts to make a world. Wipee's grandmother in the village knew that long ago.

Shotgun Marriage

Yasothorn is a rather dull province in the north-east. It is nothing much, being only on the way to more interesting places; it has nothing much, apart from a rocket festival once a year. People tend to stay there because they have to; given a choice they usually opt out.

But Yasothorn was shaken by a drama one January, which involved even the provincial governor, and brought a swarm of reporters from the capital who found the mixture of guns, love, temples and teachers irresistible news.

Let us start at the beginning, with one of the two central characters. Name: Nikkom Pongyai. Sex: male. Age: 33. Place of birth: Yasothorn (of course). Profession: secondary school teacher. Education: Mahasarakam Teacher's College. Marital status: ah, well, when this story begins, single, but it will have changed by the time it ends.

And apart from these dry facts, what else can we learn about Nikkom? The most striking thing about his character was his determination; once he decided on something, he achieved it. That was in part how he managed to get to a teacher's college, for he was only an ordinary student

Shotgun Marriage

at school (cynics might say that brilliant students never went to the teacher's college in any case, but went straight to university in Bangkok if they could afford it). He majored in physical education, and had the frame to go with it; taller than average, well-built, good-looking with a dark squarish face, almost Khmer in its outlines. But he was someone who brooked no obstacles, and was so direct in his dealings with people that many, until they realised his total sincerity, were rather shocked.

He was a good teacher in Wat Dorn School in the district of Sai Moon. His official salary was minimal, but he managed to make some extra money by coaching tennis in the *amphur muang*, the main town a few kilometres down the road. He taught the kids to swim in the local river; north-easterners usually could not, being largely without waterways.

He did not have enough to supplement the income of his parents, both minor civil servants in a government office in nearby Srisaket, but they did not expect anything or need anything either. He was an example to his younger brother, Nat, a more pliant person who followed in his footsteps and also became a teacher, though he preferred to teach Thai and he eventually joined the same school as Nikkom.

Our other principal character can also be summarised like a Ministry of the Interior statistic. Name: Salaya Boonprasert. Sex: female. Age: 15. Profession: secondary school student.

You would have guessed the marriage bit already, of course. No prizes for that. But, oh, the scandal of the

Bight of Bangkok

affair. For Nikkom assiduously wooed Salaya for months. He could easily have been a ladies' man, but he led a blameless life, sharing a rented house with his brother, never going down into what passed for the town and its standard fleshpots, always on time, always correct in his grading sheets, ever willing to take on extra school chores like supervising the lunch lines.

He was also, surprisingly, totally inexperienced in the ways of the world. He had never joined the others in trips to the local brothel; he had no fleeting affairs. Indeed, Nat started to tease Nikkom, saying that he would end up marrying before him if he did not get a move on.

From watching Salaya at a distance and observing her closely, he knew she was to be his girl. He asked Nat what he thought of her.

"Who? Salaya? The rather dark girl with the pretty face?"

"Yes, her."

"She seems all right. Why?"

Nikkom did not reply at once. "Just wondered," he said, after a long pause.

That pause made Nat wonder. Nikkom had never asked his opinion about any female before, student or other. So he quickly came back. "Surely you're not getting fond of her? You could almost be her father."

"Hardly. There's 17 years difference in our ages."

"Precisely," Nat answered. The subject was dropped.

Nikkom started to go out at nights, for walks, or so he said. Nat had a fairly good idea he was not going walking alone. But he never returned very late, and Nat was careful to observe his dress, which was always decent.

Shotgun Marriage

"Nikkom, please be careful," he said one night. "I think I know what you are up to. It isn't wise."

"But I love her," was all he got for a reply.

Nat knew Nikkom's character well enough. There was nothing he could do to stop the affair. It would have to take its course. But he feared for the inevitable storm when the scandal broke.

It broke sooner than he bargained for. Nikkom went missing for a week from the school at the same time as Salaya. He turned up one morning, wearing a black imitation leather jacket, sunglasses, and jeans just as she was coming into the temple compound to return to school. In one hand he carried a grenade, in the other, a .38 calibre pistol. Dangling from the pocket of his jeans was a pair of police handcuffs, which he took out and quickly, the moment he caught hold of her, locked one half on her right wrist, and putting the other half on his left wrist, leaving the right hand free to wield the pistol. Her friends were aghast, and ran off to call the headmaster and the other teachers, while all the other students gathered around the couple.

"We are going to get married," was all Nikkom said. Salaya was silent, but not resisting.

The headmaster and the teachers elbowed their way through the crowd in the temple compound. "Kru Nikkom, have you gone mad?" the startled headmaster asked. "Give me those weapons at once. You know they are dangerous. Someone could easily be killed."

"I am sorry, *acharn*, but I will not. Not before we are legally married."

"Married! But she's still a schoolgirl! And you are her teacher!"

"But I love her, and she loves me. We want to get married."

The girls looked at each other and grinned slyly, thoroughly enjoying the scene; the boys dug each other's ribs in delight. This was so much better than those boring lessons. Why could it not happen every day! The headmaster could see that the public spectacle was setting a bad example, and asked the two to go into his office with the other teachers. Nikkom kept everyone at a distance with his pistol.

"No nonsense, *acharn*. We get married, or I shoot. Or pull the plug on the grenade and we both disappear. You will then be the cause of our deaths."

The headmaster was at his wits end, and muttered to another teacher to call the police quickly. They soon came; Sai Moon was not a big place, and Wat Dorn was right in the middle of it. They were as confused as the headmaster when they saw the lovers, held together by handcuffs, the pistol and the grenade in Nikkom's hands.

They were still more confused when Salaya announced she needed to go to the toilet. The performance in allowing the two to leave and return, chained to each other, ready with instruments of war, was incredible. The police were all for making a quick dash to get at Nikkom's arms, but the headmaster dissuaded them.

"Don't try. He's a very determined young man. He means what he says and will really pull the pin on that grenade if you try anything. Don't." The police gave way

Shotgun Marriage

to his better judgement.

So the chained couple returned. But the news had got around. The district head had come, had informed the governor, who had decided he had better try to settle the problem and came in person, having, with some reason, little faith in the ability of the district head to resolve any issue of importance.

The police saluted smartly as the governor's car arrived in the temple compound and the governor made his way to the headmaster's office. Salaya tried to give him the traditional mark of respect, the *wai*, but with one hand handcuffed to another holding a grenade, she gave up the attempt and just curtseyed.

"Now, young man, be sensible. What on earth do you think you're doing?"

"I am trying to get married to this girl."

"Why?"

"Because I love her. And because she loves me."

The governor looked sternly at the young girl. "Do you love him, as he says?"

Salaya was too shy and overcome by the occasion to reply verbally. She just nodded, and looked at the ground.

"Then why did you not ask her parents for their permission, if that is the case?"

Nikkom answered, "Her father is dead. I did ask her mother. She refused."

The local police chief came up to the governor and whispered in his ear, "That's true, sir. Her mother had lodged a complaint that the teacher raped her daughter, and she wants 200,000 baht damages."

Bight of Bangkok

"Is she crazy?" the governor asked the police chief. "That's more than what the boy would earn as a teacher in a lifetime."

"We tried to compromise. Kru Nikkom denies rape, and has already offered her 30,000 baht as a dowry, but the offer was rejected."

"The woman's a fool then," was all the governor said.

He then addressed the handcuffed couple, trying to reason with them. "All right, it seems you love each other. But the girl is very young, Nikkom. Don't you think she should be allowed to finish her education first?"

"She is finishing in a month's time, sir, at the end of this school year. Her mother won't let her study any more. She has already taken her exams."

The governor tried another line. "Now, maybe you are acting like this because you were not careful. Babies come when they are not always expected . . . ."

Nikkom rather brusquely interrupted the dignified governor. "Salaya is not pregnant, sir. We just want to get married."

The session went on for forty minutes, the governor trying to get Nikkom to hand over the weapons and set Salaya free. He refused. The governor decided to let others try, and went outside the room. Nat then had a go, along with several other teachers ending with the same result. Nikkom was adamant. Marriage, or death by the grenade.

The head of the temple, Phrakru Piriya, Salaya's mother, Prapaiporn, the governor and the headmaster then all came in, all tried for another good half hour to get Nikkom to free the girl he loved. They promised not to hurt him if he agreed to release her.

Shotgun Marriage

"I shall let her go only if you agree to our wedding and hand over a marriage certificate."

"But this is monstrous," cried Mrs Prapaiporn. "This is denying people their liberty."

"We love each other," was Nikkom's only reply.

The governor would have liked a private discussion with Salaya, but circumstances made it impossible. He therefore spoke publicly. "Salaya, do you wish to marry this man, yes or no?"

"Yes," came the timid reply.

He turned to her mother. "Unusual as the circumstances may seem, I see no alternative but to agreeing to their request."

"But she is so young," her mother started to say.

"My wife was 16 when she married me," said the governor. This put paid to that particular line. He called over the district head.

"Go and get the person who registers marriages from the district office. We must settle this once and for all."

His orders were instantly obeyed. The cringing official came, register in hand. "Start writing out the certificate. Phrakru Piriya, please perform the usual offices. We shall all go into the temple as witnesses. Then we shall come into this office and tie the *sai sin* threads round their wrists. A pity about the handcuffs."

"Nikkom will take them off for that, if we have the certificate first," volunteered Salaya.

"And what about the gun? And the grenade?"

"I will hand those over to you when we have the certificate."

At this, Salaya thought quickly. "No. Only if no charges are brought against him."

"That's impossible. Look at the example he has set. Why, everyone will be going around with guns and grenades to marry whoever they want."

The police chief muttered under his breath, "They go around with guns and grenades anyway, and there's not much we can do to stop them."

"Then I shall ask him to use the grenade to kill us all," said Salaya, firmly.

"That is blackmail, young lady." Salaya appeared unmoved by the governor's words. He was astonished that one so young could be so determined. "They will make a formidable couple," he thought, but only said rather weakly, anxious to end the whole affair, "All right. No charges for taking a hostage, carrying offensive weapons, threatening behaviour and public disorder, given the very special circumstances. But the weapons must be handed over to the chief of police."

"As soon as we have the certificate," promised Nikkom.

The ceremony took place as he ordered. Nikkom pointed his gun throughout. With the certificate signed and presented, Nikkom and Salaya smiled shyly at each other. They were man and wife.

"Now, release her," ordered the governor. From one of the pockets in his jeans Nikkom found the key to the handcuffs and sprang the lock. He gave the handcuffs, the grenade and the pistol to the police chief, who looked at the weapons carefully. "Hmm . . . ," he said, "there are no bullets in the pistol. Which is not oiled either. And the grenade is an empty casing."

"True," said Nikkom, "I did not want anyone to be hurt."

They walked hand in hand to the headmaster's office, where students had hastily arranged stools and a table for the thread tying. Prapaiporn's hands trembled in fury as she picked up the white threads and tied one each round the wrists of Salaya and her new son-in-law, and thought of the money she had failed to extract from Kru Nikkom. She gave not a single thought to her daughter's radiant happiness.

"Well then, I suppose I should congratulate you," said the governor. "But your headmaster says you will be charged for absence without permission from your post of duty as a government official for one week. That will mean a reprimand and a pay deduction."

Nikkom was not in the least worried about that; he had got what he wanted. But he had not bargained for the publicity his action caused. Reporters came from nearby Ubol to interview him, a television team from the capital was sent up to find him and film his school, Salaya, Prapaiporn, the headmaster, Phrakru Piriya, the Sai Moon police chief, even the governor (who declined the honour). While the headmaster managed to make some money from the publicity and felt it brought fame to his school, he felt it came rather too close to notoriety. He quietly and speedily arranged for Nikkom's transfer to another district at the other end of the province, with the agreement of the governor and the representative of the Ministry of Education in Yasothorn. And, at the governor's suggestion, the matter of the pay deduction and the reprimand were dropped.

"Let it be our wedding gift," he said.

The Drink-Mixing School

In the free-for-all that passes for vocational education in Bangkok, a number of rather shady institutions operate alongside very respectable ones. One of the former was what we shall call the Dusit Drink-Mixing School. That was however, not its real name, even though it happened to be in the Dusit district of the capital.

This less than venerable establishment was set up two years previously by one Poonperm Silapapakdee, who was just thirty and who had completed primary education. He had subsequently made a fair amount of money by means most suspected of being less than legal. His school, which consisted of two rooms, one teacher, and a dimwit but a glamorous female assistant, was on the fourth floor of a grubby shop-house in a street in which the busy Rajawat market was located.

Surprisingly, given its lack of visual appeal, the school attracted students; people were often desperate for jobs, and one of the baits the school held out in its prospectus was the certainty of a job on completion of the course.

The prospectus was a masterpiece. Of deceit. Poonperm was attributed all sorts of bogus degrees (among others, M.Sc. Horvard in Alcoholic Chemistry, Ph.D. Southern

The Drink-Mixing School

Alaska, in Human Relations), though the qualifications of his one teacher, Dhiarthai, were more truthfully listed as "Legal Studies, Ramkamhaeng University" (in fact he had not completed his part-time course in law). The prospectus described in extensive detail the course contents, all the things the students would learn, and ended with lavish words of praise from supposed former students to the school for it having found them such wonderful jobs in various first-class hotels, some even abroad.

Sittichai Kamloi, while eating a bowl of noodles one night by the market, was handed a prospectus by the dimwit assistant who went around distributing them to anyone who looked in need of a job. He read its contents carefully. It was not expensive, really — five hundred baht for a total of twenty lessons, usually spread over two months but which could be taken "in an accelerated mode" if preferred. All classes were held in the evenings, at 6.30 or 8.30 p.m., each lasting two hours, so they did not interfere with looking for a job in the daytime.

Like many others, Sittichai had come to the capital to find a job. The rains had failed, there was nothing to do on the farm, and no money. Like many others he had not succeeded in finding work. He had offered his services at petrol pumps, but they preferred young boys, because they did not argue when paid much less than the official minimum wage. He was already 23, rather short and thin, so he was not likely to be taken on for coolie work. He had no money, but he had a sister who cleaned and washed in different apartments in the Soi Aree area. He persuaded her to lend him the money for the course.

"It guarantees you a job," he said. "Look, it says so here, in the prospectus."

His sister, Noi, was all for peace and quiet, and being younger could hardly refuse her elder brother his request, and gave a little more to keep him at arm's length for a week or so. At least she had a job, several in fact, though she had to run from flat to flat and work incredible hours to earn enough to live on and pay the rent on the room she shared with her brother and a few others from the same impoverished up-country village.

So he started the course. He had not realised that the "course book" was an extra fifty baht. It had crude drawings of glasses of different shapes and sizes filled with various liquids. There were long lists of names, in Thai and English, of all sorts of cocktails he had to learn by heart: gimlet, martini, manhattan, eggnog, screwdriver... Unfortunately it did not say that the mode for these concoctions was the 1930s and hardly anyone drank them now.

The classes were small, with usually about five or six others. They held bottles of cold tea pretending they contained whisky and poured the contents over imaginary ice cubes placed in the glass with real tongs. They learned how to uncork a bottle of wine with an empty bottle and a cork that needed frequent replacement. They were supposed, as part of the curriculum, to know something of all the different wines available, but were told by Acharn Dhiarthai that they did not have to bother about this, because very few people could afford wine, so few asked for it. The course tended to concentrate on cocktails, whisky and brandy.

The Drink-Mixing School

"That's what most people drink now," Acharn Dhiarthai said, authoritatively.

During the day, Sittichai studied his course book intensively. He wanted to be absolutely sure of being worthy of the job promised him. The one thing his education had taught him was rote-learning, and he soon had the names of all the drinks off by heart. He practised carefully so as not to spill the precious contents of the dummy bottles, and got the right angle and controlled speed for pouring out imaginary beer so that the froth did not flow all over the place.

Having opted for the "accelerated mode", Sittichai finished his course quite quickly. There was a final examination, consisting entirely of multiple-choice questions but where the answers were so obvious that no one could go wrong. There was a small ceremony, at which he and a couple of others were presented certificates by Poonperm, dressed as usual in his smart business suit and sporting his huge diamond ring.

He waxed eloquent. "I am always proud on occasions like this, to see the results of your endeavours. We admire and esteem those who had tried and succeeded. We wish you all success in the future as you go out into the world, and we hope you will cherish and respect the start the Dusit Drink-Mixing School has given you." He was never at loss for a cliché or two.

"Now I would like to see you in the next couple of days so that we can fix things for the job," he added.

Ah, the job. Sittichai was afraid he might have forgotten. They all made appointments in an otherwise empty diary

Bight of Bangkok

with the dimwit girl to see Poonperm.

Poonperm did not show up for the appointment he fixed for Sittichai. Nor for the next one. Sittichai remonstrated with the dimwit, who was unmoved. She had no job to offer him. When Poonperm failed to turn up a third time, he barged into one of "Acharn" Dhiarthai's evening classes.

"Where's that boss of yours, Khun Poonperm? I finished the course, got my certificate, three times I made an appointment to fix getting the job you promised, and he never turns up."

"I think he may have gone up-country," Dhiarthai said.

"Then I'll wait for him to come back," said Sittichai.

Dimwit opened her mouth, suppressing a yawn. "He may be gone some time."

Sittichai began to realise he might have been conned, losing face in the process. And so had all the others. He went back to his room, fuming. When his sister came back from her work, exhausted, she expressed no surprise. "Try on your own," was all she could suggest.

He did, with no success. In Bangkok, you need connections. He had none. He went back to the Dusit School. No job of course, and no sign of Poonperm.

He waited outside the shop-house towards the end of the month for the owner to come to his office, calculating Poonperm had to pay his employees. He came in one morning about ten, besuited and diamond ring flashing. He did not notice Sittichai in wait; even if he had, he would not have recognised him.

Sittichai followed him up the dank stairs at a distance.

The Drink-Mixing School

Dimwit saw him and tried to prevent him entering Poonperm's office, but Sittichai was stronger than her. Slamming the door shut behind him and propping a chair against it, he pulled out a gun.

"Give me that job you promised me!" he ordered.

"What job?"

"You know. You finish the course and you get a job. So you said."

Poonperm looked nervously down the barrel of the gun. "The employment situation is very difficult now . . . ."

"A promise is a promise, where I come from," he shouted. "You get me a job, OK. No job, and that's the end of you."

Poonperm tried to pick up the telephone. Sittichai stopped him quickly. "No funny business. A job!" he screamed.

"You shitty little runt, you coyboy, you mud-soaked buffalo," began Poonperm. "You think you can come in here and threaten me with your toy gun. A job in a bar? Why you're not capable of a job in the toilets."

Sittichai was not going to stand for that. "So, that's what you think. Right." He fired straight at Poonperm, with a direct shot between the eyes. It was no toy gun. Poonperm slumped to the floor, blood and brains splattering everywhere.

The next move was not planned. Sittichai had got his revenge. But he could hear a commotion downstairs, and people coming up, no doubt summoned by Dimwit. He threw down the gun, secured the chair, ran up another flight of stairs, wrenched open the door onto the roof, and fastened it as securely as he could. He then ran to the edge of the building, looking down into the street. A crowd was gathering at the entrance to the building.

It was not long before the door to the roof was forced open by several burly people, no doubt brought in from the market.

"If you try to get me, I'll throw myself down."

"Go on then," one of them said. "You haven't got the guts."

They were wrong. As they advanced on him, Sittichai jumped. He broke his legs on landing, but the pain did not last long. He was almost immediately run over by a speeding bus.

His body was collected by a charitable foundation, to be picked up some days after by Noi. Poonperm's body was immediately taken to a fashionable hospital nearby but there was no hope. His diamond ring was missing when he was admitted.

Welcome Home

Rat had lived all his life in a village near Bua Yai, which has no claim to fame other than being a railway junction of a very third world kind, in the middle of the uninteresting Korat plateau in the north-east. Life in the village was harsh; drought was a perpetual worry and existence was hand-to-mouth. His wife, Mai, managed to supplement their meagre income from the sale of rice by making and selling a few lengths of traditional *mat-miee* patterned silk cloth, raising the silkworms and doing the entire production herself, like most of the other no-longer-so-young women in the village. They had four children, all grown up and out at work; not in the village or even in Bua Yai, where of course there was no work. The eldest boy had managed, after several failed attempts to stay in the capital, to get a job in Korat, and the other three were all in Bangkok, the two girls worked in a textile factory and the youngest boy served sandwiches and snacks in a late-night bar of dubious respectability.

Rat was hard-working, and had an additional skill to rice-growing; he was an able carpenter, often in demand to assist in house-building in the village. He had only one vice, if such it was — he was addicted to watching television in the evening, and to the scenes of high life and conspicuous consumption that poured out from the screen. He would like to see something of the world before he died and there was no way he could do that except by work. He heard of someone in a nearby village who had recently returned from working overseas, and decided, without telling Mai, to go and find out what it was like.

"At first it's terrible," the returnee told him. "You have to work every day, seven days a week, for anything from 10 to 14 hours a day, in all weathers. And you have to carry on like this for seven months in order to pay off the agent sending you abroad."

"Why, how much does it cost?" Rat asked.

"About 40,000 baht," he was told. "They find you a job, get your passport, get your work permit, arrange the visa, provide the air ticket, and so on."

"I hadn't thought of flying. Isn't it dangerous?"

"No more than driving to Korat on the main road. Maybe less."

"Was it cold?" Rat had seen enough of snowy scenes of Alpine resorts on television to be worried about that. The north-east could be cold in December and January too, as the winds from China howled over the featureless plateau, but at least it never snowed.

"Well, I was in Singapore, and the climate is much the same as here, except that it never gets cold and it rains a lot. But some people who have been to 'Sa-u', they say it can get very cold in winter. And hotter than here in summer, but the heat is very dry, not like our hot season."

Welcome Home

"How long do you have to stay?"

"Usually two years. Some people want to stay longer. But most return."

"And can you save?"

"Oh yes, if you are careful. After paying back the agent, I managed to save quite a lot. I sent money back through friends or the bank. Maybe 200,000 baht altogether. Plus a few things for the house." He gestured to the huge new television set on show in the middle of the room. Conspicuous consumption was spreading, and the size of that set made Rat green with envy.

"What did you do?"

"I was mostly working on building sites, with lots of other Thais. I used to bend metal bars and tie them up. Gradually I got quite good at it. We all got on well on the whole. But there were two problems."

"Oh?"

"First of all, almost no one apart from the Thais speaks Thai. You need English or Chinese in Singapore. And the Chinese there try to take advantage of you. So it was not much fun to go out; very occasionally a few of us would go out together, but getting back to our clapboard quarters was tough."

"Yes, I heard some minister saying his dog in Bangkok lived in better quarters."

"Maybe his dog did, but I bet his servants didn't. You stay in the same kind of place you see on any building site in this country. Not very comfortable, but good enough for a short time."

"You mentioned one other thing."

"Yes, *lai-dai*."

Rat knew all about that. It affected many males in the north-east. They would go to bed feeling normal, wake up as though in a nightmare, gasping, and die. Widow ghosts took them off, people said. The only prevention was to try and fool the ghosts by painting your fingernails and wearing dresses at night. No one could do anything about it and death when it came was sudden.

"Did many people die of that there too?"

"Yes, quite a lot. But people there say it is something to do with our diet, our ways of cooking sticky rice, and maybe worrying about debts. But if you only have the agent to pay off, and have no other debts, then you need not worry. Do you have any special skill? That's what they really want."

"I've done a lot of carpentry in my spare time, building houses and so on."

"Then you'll be taken on for sure, if you pass the medical." He thought Rat, a well-built man, would have no problems there. "You have to have an AIDS test, you know."

"A what?"

His worldly-wise neighbour explained, and how the disease was contracted.

"No worries. I have only ever known my wife."

The neighbour thought that miracles never ceased, and willingly gave Rat the name and address of the agent who had supplied him his job. Rat returned home and discussed his idea with Mai.

"But who will plant the rice in our fields?" she asked.

Welcome Home

"You can do some, and hire some labour. And rent out some of the fields too. There'll be some takers. Land is short around here."

Mai knew that well enough; it was also expensive. She would not dream of selling; sooner cut off her right hand.

So Rat wrote to the agent, was sent a form which was returned. He went to the capital for an interview, had his medical, and before too long, though having borrowed more than he had ever dreamed of from the agent, he was on his way to what his mates called "Sa-u", Saudi Arabia to the non-initiated.

The airplane journey delighted him. He felt slightly sick at first, but once he got used to it, it was rather fun. He was disappointed at only seeing clouds though. He thought he might see something else, flying saucers maybe, angels even. He kept being offered alcoholic drinks by the hostesses, but always refused. "No thanks, I don't drink. Water, please." Only later he realised why some were drinking far too much; once there, there was nothing like that to drink.

The work was indeed hard, and the hours long. There was nowhere to go and nothing to spend any money on. His ability as a carpenter pleased his bosses, and he started to do some fancy fretwork, largely to try his hand at it. His bosses liked that even more. He found them hard task-masters, but once they appreciated your worth, they were fair. His pay went up. In time he had paid off his debts to the agent, and started sending some money home.

Letters came from Bua Yai from time to time. Mai was not a great correspondent, but told him the essential things;

the fields were planted, some were rented, the children were all right. There was, as always, little rain. They had something in common, he thought when he read this. But at least there was plenty of water in "Sa-u"; they had the money to desalinate it, or dig deep wells to tap underground sources.

Rat often thought of home, of course. He was beginning to regret his two-year contract after the first year had passed. He would not stay on, though his bosses, who liked his work, wanted him to. The day eventually came when he, together with five others who had arrived at more or less the same time as he did, was able to board the airplane, lugging a fancy camera he could not work because all the instructions were in English, gifts for Mai and the kids, as well as small presents for the neighbours, of course the inevitable huge television set, and a great deal of money, in both dinars and dollars. For his last six months he had not bothered to send any back, but saved in cash. Why pay bank charges unnecessarily?

The six of them had some trouble getting through the customs at Don Muang with their television sets. They were, after all, rather obvious. After some argument, they paid a nominal duty, and then made their way, in style by taxi, to Maw Chit bus station. There they went their different ways; one was only going as far as Korat, two were off to Sakol Nakorn, one to Prae, one to Ubol. He was the only one going to Bua Yai.

A young man about the age of his eldest son came up to buy a ticket to Bua Yai at the counter at the same time as Rat.

"Just come back from 'Sa-u'?" he asked.

Welcome Home

"Yes, been there two years."

"I was there last year. Made a lot of money driving trucks. Good experience, and good pay. Not like here. My name's Suraphon, by the way."

"Yes, the pay is all right. But I'll be glad to get home. Two years is a long time."

"I bet your wife is looking forward to your return," said Suraphon. "Two years is a long time without a husband around. Some don't like it."

"I've no trouble there."

As they had an hour or so to spare before the evening bus they were booked on was due to leave, Suraphon suggested they had something to eat together. They found a grilled chicken stand and bought some on sticks, with sticky rice. Suraphon ordered a beer. Rat as usual stuck to water.

"Tastes good to eat this again, almost like home, eh?" asked Suraphon.

"Yea," was all Rat said. He was feeling tired after the long flight, and wanted to be back in Bua Yai.

They boarded the bus, after Rat had stowed, with difficulty, his television, together with his travelling case in the bag section. Suraphon arranged with the bus hostess to swap seats with someone to sit next to Rat and to continue discussing their experiences. They chatted as they passed the airport again, and then were stuck in interminable traffic at Rangsit. The hostess served soft drinks and snacks. Slowly the lights outside got thinner, then the cabin lights went out and a video of mind-boggling stupidity was shown to the captivated audience.

Bight of Bangkok

Rat was weary, and dozed off.

He was woken with difficulty by the bus hostess. It was still dark outside, but Rat knew he must have arrived. He had a bad headache and a sore throat. He asked — words did not come out easily — what happened to the person who was travelling with him.

"He told me he was going to take a *tuk-tuk* when we got to Sida." That was some 16 kilometres before Bua Yai, still on the main road.

"I thought he was going all the way to Bua Yai," said Rat.

He looked down at the grip he was carrying which was on the floor. It was open. He fished inside it and felt around. The new camera was missing. So was his passport. And so was the envelope with all the dollars and dinars he had been saving for the past six months.

He jumped up, nearly knocking his head on the rack above. "I've been robbed!" he shouted.

The hostess was alarmed. She was about to go off duty. "Who would have robbed you?"

"The man next to me. He said his name was Suraphon."

A person sitting behind him said, "Go straight to the police. If he got off at Sida he cannot be far away. They all have radios now."

Rat followed his suggestion immediately as the bus came to a halt a minute or so later and he had extracted his TV set and travelling case. The police were cooperative but not hopeful. "He could have gone in any direction, you know. But most likely operates out of Bangkok, and so will have gone there. How do you think he got your money?"

Welcome Home

"I think he put something in my drink in the bus. Or maybe before, when we had some food together at Maw Chit."

"So he got into conversation with you there, did he?"

"Yes."

"All right. We'll get in touch if there's any news. How are you going to get home?"

Rat pulled out a one dollar bill from his pocket. "That's all I've got left." The policeman gave him twenty-five baht and kept the note. Rat loaded his television set, his small travelling case and largely empty grip onto a converted motorbike with a few seats at the back, and went the seven kilometres to his village as dawn was breaking.

Gone were his savings of six months; he might just as well not have bothered to work at all for that period. Gone was his passport too, but he did not care about that. He was not a person who attached a great deal of importance to money, but was bitter at being cheated, and by a fellow Thai too.

Mai greeted him as though he had left that morning. The neighbours were impressed by the size of the television. They were angry when they heard of his misfortune on the night bus.

"It's always the same. Those city slickers. They think we only exist to give them a living." No one in the village stole, or would dream of doing so.

Alone that night, Rat wept, for the first time in many years. Mai consoled him. "It doesn't matter. We can live without it. You can work all our fields again as you used to. We still have the money you managed to send back after you'd paid the agent."

"But the last six months . . ."

"Forget it," was Mai's advice. "We shall never see that again."

She was not absolutely right. About a week after his return, a couple of policemen on motorbikes came to the village and asked for Rat's house.

A crowd of onlookers quickly gathered. Nothing was secret in the village.

"Khun Rat, we have your passport for you."

"Oh, what happened?"

They explained that they caught someone, whose name was not Suraphon but Preecha, on a bus going back to Bangkok early that morning, before it even got to Korat. He also had some sleeping pills, which after questioning he admitted to buying at Chatuchat Park for 100 baht each. Apparently he and his accomplices would sometimes follow people on arrival at the airport from overseas contracts, but mostly hung around the bus station looking for likely victims. He had 4,000 baht in Thai currency and 50,000 baht in dinars and dollars on him. He admitted having stolen it, and was one of a gang preying on north-easterners.

Rat quickly said, "I had more than that. Double, in fact."

"We thought you might have more. But this money Preecha says, comes from several people. You were not the only one. He says you were the sixth person that week."

"I might have been, but that money was mine."

"That's what we thought. But it looks as though you

Welcome Home

might have to share it with the other victims, if Preecha sticks to his story."

"What about my camera?"

"No sign of that. We reckon he had someone waiting to meet him, part of his gang, at Sida, who went in another direction, or maybe on another bus and was not picked up, with some of the money and the camera."

Mai, who had been silent up to then, asked, "Well, what will happen?"

"We need to investigate further. Check up on others Preecha admitted to robbing. Try to find the rest of the gang. It will take time."

It did. And presumably money. Four months later, Rat received 5,000 baht through the police as his share of the money recovered.

But he had his TV, which looked good, but unfortunately worked on a different system from the one in "Sa-u", so it showed nothing there. And he had his passport, which would never be used again. And his memories of his welcome home in Bangkok.